GOTHIC BLUE BOOK IV
The Folklore Edition

Edited by
Cynthia (Cina) Pelayo & Gerardo Pelayo

DEDICATION

We dedicate this Gothic Blue Book to the Nobel Prize winning novelist and short story writer Gabriel García Márquez. His works of magical realism, fiction that integrates fantasy into realistic settings, such as *One Hundred Years of Solitude* have been read worldwide. Márquez' works, which are often romantic and dramatic and set in sleepy towns, are not horror, but are full of magic. Garcia's writing is also full of surrealism, and the occasional ghost and steps dripping in blood.

"Nothing resembles a person as much as the way he dies."
- Gabriel García Márquez (March 6, 1927-April 17, 2014) *Love in the Time of Cholera*

CONTENTS

Aisha Abram	Friend Of The Family	9
Jay Bonansinga	Bivouac	12
Bruce Boston	Collected Poems	22
Chad P. Brown	Bones Chimes	30
Tara Cleves	The Butterfly Gardener	39
M. Frank Darbe	Parcel Post	48
Lance Davis	Spooklight	56
Nicole DeGennaro	Making Friends	58
James Dorr	School Nights	65
Christina Glenn	Down By The River	67
Agustin Guerrero	Hunting The Devil	69
Emma Hinge	Seaside Bound	75
Kelly Hoolihan	Bus Stop	81
K. Trap Jones	Where It All Started	85
Kerry G. S. Lipp	Fairborn, Ohio Where Trains And Ghosts Still Run	91
Sean Logan	The Crawling Man	97
David Massengill	Looking Glass	103
Edward J. McFadden III	Lost Days	110
Meredith Morgenstern	Atheists In The Cemetery	117
g. Elmer Munson	Family Business	125
Lawrence Salani	The Cursed	133
Cathy Smith	Gifts From A Grim Godfather	135

THE FOLKLORE EDITION

INTRODUCTION

Gothic Blue Books were descendants of chapbooks that peaked in popularity between the 1800s and early 1900s. They were abridgements of Gothic novels, and they were very cheap which lead to their nicknames of "Shilling Shockers" or "Sixpenny Shockers." These miniature horror tales took readers on a tour through dark castles, cursed abbeys, and homes haunted with ghosts and demons. These stories were not welcomed by the literati. In fact, many readers at the time frowned upon the consumption of ghost stories. Still, these stories were adored by many, so much so that few copies remain as they were made with inexpensive paper and after being read and reread their pages withered away. Our attempt at reviving this tradition is to bring you a hint of the traditional Gothic horror found in the original Gothic Blue Books. Of course, our work comes with modern twists.

Within folklore one finds stories of legend, belief, history and more. Within folklore we also find traditions and cultures of a group, and within this collection we find many tales common in America and throughout the Americas.

American folklore, the kind that aims to chill, often includes tales of warning. Within these pages we find a woman who comes terribly close to a killer, a scientist whose work devastates humanity, and a recluse who will kill to keep his family secret alive. In this collection, we also find familiar tales, tales that have been told and retold – mysterious lights over a canyon that lead us to wonder the validity of UFOs, the legend of La Llorona, the murderous Weeping Woman, the monstrous Jersey Devil, the vampires of the Ursuline Convent in New Orleans, and of course a meeting with Godfather Death.

We hope that you enjoy this, our fourth Gothic Blue Book – The Folklore Edition featuring new fiction by Jay Bonansinga and poetry by Bruce Boston.

Cynthia (cina) Pelayo
Gravedigger/Publisher
Burial Day Books

THE FOLKLORE EDITION

FRIEND OF THE FAMILY
Aisha Abram

Aisha Abram writes fiction from her home near St. Louis. She is a former reporter who traded fact for fiction. An MFA graduate of Lindenwood University, Aisha's first professional post was as a staff writer for a bi-weekly Missouri newspaper. Her short fiction recently appeared in the February 2014 edition of *Hello Horror*, an online literary journal. She has a passion for all things horror and continues to write about things that scare her.

Sasha liked the dead. They were good coworkers—they never lied, never gossiped, never said she looked fat, never wanted to borrow fifty bucks.

Strangers always gave her a second look when she told them she worked for the county coroner. It really was the perfect job. She had few restrictions. She took lunch when she wanted; read, surfed the internet, and talked on the phone.

Halloween was the only holiday that bothered Sasha. The prank calls were worse. The coroner thought it funny to put a Frankenstein mask on one of the cadavers. Again.

The coroner was a recluse who preferred to do his work in private. When he didn't have a customer on the table, he used his time to watch porn on the internet, and sneak out the door for hour-long cigarette breaks.

The coroner was a connoisseur when it came to tobacco. Marlboro had a nice woodsy quality while Pall Mall was smooth and pithy. He found that Camels paired well with a candied apple snatched from the nurses' lounge.

He was forced to the area outside the lounge not long after funeral homes complained of ashes and cigarette butts stuffed between the deep Y-stitch of each autopsy.

Sasha's job was to file the paperwork and help with the identifications. These were done with the use of a video monitor. Sasha would wheel the selected gurney out under a video monitor, and uncover the face of the deceased for a person in another room watching a video monitor. This way there were fewer "scenes."

The coroner hated the "scenes" and did his best to be on a break when the identifier was there.

Sasha didn't like the visitors, not because of the emotion they projected, but because they took all the fun out of her guesses. Sasha always guessed who the person was in life.

There was the young, petite waif girl who came in wearing a tattered pink leotard. Sasha imagined her a prima ballerina. An older man with sideburns and a "Heartbreak Hotel" tattoo was an aged Elvis.

The girl was a heroin junkie; the man was a plumber.

"We've got a big case just came in," the coroner said, on his way to another smoke break. "A regular four-for-one special. Two adults, plus boy and girl. Head on collision on the highway. It'll be a while before the authorities notify next of kin, so they may be here for a while before we get a direct ID."

Sasha nodded a yes, barely glancing up from her internet cat video. The coroner crossed the room, cigarettes in hand.

"I'm gonna get some fresh air," he said. "No car fire with this one. At least they're not crispy, I hate the crispy ones. Couldn't eat bacon for a week after that last one."

Sasha returned to the internet.

"Excuse me," a voice said. Sasha looked up from the screen.

A tall thin man stood just a foot away.

"I'm sorry, I didn't hear you come in. Can I help you?"

Sasha noticed the man's attire was simple. He wore a crisp black pant and jacket. His clothes were freshly pressed but his face was a mass of wrinkles. His cheek bones were prominent giving the illusion of a starving man.

"I'm here to identify the family," he said.

"Which family?"

"The car accident, up on the highway, not too long ago. It should be two parents, a boy and a girl."

"Oh, are you related?" she said.

"I've known the family for a long time," he said.

"I'm sorry for your loss. We weren't expecting anyone for a while," she said. "Let me get the monitors set up so we can do the identifications, wait here—."

The man reached out and grabbed Sasha's arm. A cold chill went through her.

"No, Miss, wait," he said. "I want to see them, not over a monitor but in person."

"Are you sure? Most people find it hard to do identifications on the monitor, let alone in person."

The man nodded a yes.

Sasha led the man to where the four bodies lay on gurneys. She pulled back the first sheet. It was an older woman.

The man remained silent. Sasha waited for some kind of response. When none came, she covered the woman's head and lifted the second sheet. It was the man.

Sasha's visitor remained silent.

"Is this the right family?" she said.

The man shook his head, and his pallid skin looked skeletal in the fluorescent lights. His sunken eyes deepened into black pools.

"Shall we continue?" he said.

Sasha moved to where the smaller figures were lying and uncovered the first, a girl.

The man sighed and leaned forward. Sasha caught a glimpse of something shiny on his chest. As he leaned towards the girl a silver cross on a silver chain slid from his jacket. He quickly tucked it back in and motioned for Sasha to continue.

Sasha uncovered the final victim, a boy no older than five. She covered him again.

"That's them," he said.

"I'm sorry for your loss," she said. "Come up to my desk and we'll fill out the paperwork."

The man turned to follow Sasha to the front. Sasha slid into her desk and turned around. The man was gone.

Sasha searched the office rooms but there was no sign of the man.

He must've gone out to get some air, she thought. Sasha's eyes scanned the room again. This time she noticed dark spots on the linoleum.

Dots of blood shimmered along the floor, in perfect position with which the man had walked.

"Did I miss anything?" The coroner's voice boomed as he walked in the door.

"Yeah it's about the family we need to identify…"

"I know, nurses were talking about it," he said. "Ambulance drivers too. Told me the accident was a hit and run. They think the other driver must have gotten hurt too. Too much blood at the scene."

Sasha turned her head towards the four figures and the droplets. Outside, she could faintly hear the hum of the highway.

BIVOUAC
Jay Bonansinga

Jay Bonansinga is the New York Times bestselling author of twenty books, including the Bram Stoker Award finalist *The Black Mariah* (1994), the International Thriller Writers Award finalist *Shattered* (2007), and the wildly popular *Walking Dead* novels. Jay's work has been translated into eleven languages, and he has been called "one of the most imaginative writers of thrillers" by the *Chicago Tribune*. He lives in the Chicago area with his wife, the photographer Jill Norton, and his two teenage boys, and is currently hard at work on the next *Walking Dead* book in the Woodbury quartet. You can find Jay on-line at jaybonansinga.com.

They started before dawn.

At this altitude, the chill air, scented with pine and humus, felt electric to Jake Berman as he led his teenage daughter and her boyfriend across the parking lot and up the narrow, rutted mouth of the Mount Bleeker trailhead. The path had a difficulty factor of nine, according to park brochures, but in the silent, wee-hour darkness, the prospects of making it to the summit – eleven miles away, and nearly fifteen thousand feet above sea level – seemed to Jake to be well within their collective grasp. He bubbled with the primordial adrenaline of the marathon runner coiled and waiting for the bark of the starter pistol.

"Flashlights on," he enthused to the others as he started up the gentle incline of craggy, weed-whiskered steps. "Until the sun clears the trees, it's gonna be dark as pitch below the tree line." A pair of metallic clicks behind him and all at once, two identical beams of silver radiance danced across the palisades of birch and Englemann spruce on either side of them. "Stay close, and pace yourselves."

They strode along at a decent clip, and nobody said much of anything until the pallid light began to infuse the darkness like cream being stirred into a cup of black coffee. At first, Jake sensed the others in his peripheral vision as mere silhouettes trudging along single-file behind him – a skinny waif of an eighteen-year-old girl dressed in anachronistic black spandex and high-top sneakers, furiously chewing and snapping her bubble gum; and behind her, bringing up the rear, a morose seventeen year old boy with a veil of sapphire-dyed hair dangling down across his acne scarred face.

Jake was no super model himself – a gangly man in his mid-forties with the bespectacled face of a mid-level bureaucrat or corporate accountant, his slender, knob-kneed legs swimming now in designer label cargo shorts that were two sizes too big. Embittered by divorce, hounded by a wide array of neuroses, he was the sole heir to the Berman-Klein defense contract fortune. And now, in his enormous clod-hopper boots and store-bought backpack, Jake Berman gave off an air of softness and fecklessness, like an overgrown child playing dress-up with his father's mountain climbing gear.

As the group slowly ascended the leprous trail, the day gradually dawned. A nearby stream babbled its genial white noise, and larks and finches began to chitter in the treetops. Jake Berman smiled to himself. He sorely needed this respite from the pressure-cooker of a year he had been having at the lab, and as the light chased the shadows from the adjacent woods, he felt magnificent. He filled his lungs with cold, pristine air and commented, more to himself than anyone else, "Fantastic…isn't it?"

"I'm just wondering why it wouldn't be *just* as fantastic if we had gotten up at a normal hour?"

"Sarah, I told you a million times, the storms roll in at noon every day so we have to start this early in order to make it to the summit before the weather turns."

"I think it's kinda *rad*, starting this early."

"Shut up, Todd."

"Okay, both of you just take a deep breath and try to enjoy yourselves."

They put another half a mile of trail behind them, ascending to nearly ten thousand feet without saying much of anything to each other. Jake tried to concentrate on the scenic beauty around them, the otherworldly calm, and the convivial morning sun filtering down through the high foliage as they trundled along with their heavy, jangling backpacks. He tried to drive away the residual stress of work still pinching his chest – the debacle of recent weeks with the government inspection, the rumors of containment vessel failures, and the scuttlebutt bouncing around the facility that Jake's project was being shut down. Very few locals had ever even *heard* of The Defense Intelligence Agency's Ames Research Facility, let alone *seen* it – it was well hidden in the barren hinterlands north of Denver, camouflaged as an innocuous power station or sewage treatment center – but now, Jake feared, it was about to become a hot topic on everything from Wolf

Blitzer's Situation Room to TMZ.

At last, the voice of Todd McFetridge, ace bike messenger and avid cannabis user, broke the tranquil yet somewhat awkward silence. "Okay, so… this dude in the Wagon Wheel bar last night? He was going on and on about how this mountain is supposed to be like…cursed or something."

"Todd —"

"No, no…Sarah, I'm serious. I looked it up. At one time, all this land used to belong to like…the Arapaho nation. This was like…sacred ground. Dude, we're like tromping through their church. Or their graveyard. *We're walking on their graves*, is more like it."

"Okay, let's save the ghost stories for the campfire," Jake admonished. "I think it's time we took a little water break, what do you think?"

They paused near an enormous, scabrous boulder half embedded in the ground, shrugged off their packs, and dug into their granola bars and water bottles. They didn't hear the sirens building down in the lower elevations, the cacophony of crashes and screams blending with the wail of first responders. They didn't notice the first hints of anomalous odors wafting up from the towns and cities surrounding the campus of the secret DIA lab. They didn't even make note of the odd silence that had befallen the higher elevations.

They were far too engrossed in their challenging hike to notice that the world had already begun to change, and they were already trapped.

They made good time that day in the hours before the text came through.

By 11:00 a.m. they had reached the 'tree line' – a demarcation point at which the trees imperceptibly shrivel to tiny saplings, and the vegetation gives way to the scrawny, low-to-the-ground scrub of the alpine environment – a vast ecosystem that wreathes the jagged front range of the Rocky Mountains. Above the tree line, the air gets so thin the lungs pang, and the sun fries exposed skin to deep scarlet in a matter of minutes. From this point on, the cathedral of Mount Bleeker's summit loomed naked and unadorned before them, a giant pinnacle of red granite scraping the agitated clouds, daring anyone with the *cojones* to just *try* and climb this *monster*. Sweat had broken out down the small of Jake Berman's back, and he had removed his fleece jacket and tied it around his waist, despite the fact that the raw wind had picked up, and any perspiration that had the temerity to break out was immediately freeze-dried. Sarah marched along with her denim shirt bound around her head like a turban, and Todd trundled dutifully behind her with his shirt open to expose the spider-web tattoo scrawled between his emaciated pectorals.

Jake was about to call another rest stop when his cell phone – up to this point a useless digital appendix suffering from a complete lack of service – began to let out a telltale, tinny burst of Vivaldi's 'Four Seasons,' which signaled an incoming text. Jake paused and looked at the display, and behind him Sarah paused, and behind her Todd paused, breathing hard, his hands on his bony hips. "What is it?"

"Oh…no."

For a brief instant, the feeble exhalation of words that had escaped from Jake's lungs made the two other hikers become very still, almost instinctively, as the alpine gusts tossed their artificially tinted hair. They waited. And stared. And waited.

"Oh…no, no, no-no-no-no." Jake clicked the sleep button and returned the phone to his pocket. He looked up at the others as a sleepwalker might look at a person who has just awakened him. "It's nothing."

"Dad, don't lie."

He looked at his daughter. "We have to go back."

"Um…yeah…*what?*" Todd McFetridge took a step closer, leaned an elbow on his girlfriend's shoulder, and cocked a bewildered look at the man. "I thought we were, like, making good time."

Jake Berman was already breezing past them in his chunky, clomping boots and knobby knees. He swallowed his terror and acted as calm and collected as humanly possible under the circumstances. "Yes…um…we'll come back…I promise…it's just…it seems there's been a…it's an emergency."

The two teenagers gave each other a glance and a shrug, and then followed the older man.

"Dad, Jesus…would you please slow down…who was that text from?"

"Guy at work," Jake murmured breathlessly as he scuttled down the narrow, rock-strewn trail. His heart was slamming inside his sternum. He tried his best to not appear mortified and thunderstruck. He couldn't think straight. Was he dreaming? It had to be a mistake. "They had an accident," Jake went on between labored breaths. At this elevation, even going down is an arduous task, hard on the knees, exhausting. Dehydration is a serious issue. "I have to…I have to get back before it gets…I have to get back."

They shambled toward the tree line. Stumbling over corrugations of stone, Jake could see the ridge of bald earth about a quarter mile away, below which the forest began to thicken and spread in all directions, a bosom of deep green that reached down into the valley toward the trailhead as far as the eye could see.

At this rate, they could make the parking lot by noon, maybe the town by 1:30, and then what? If what the text said were true, there was no place on earth to hide.

"Goddamnit, Dad, slow down!" Sarah's entreaty reached Jake's ears – a wobbly, trembly plea – distorted by her bumpy strides. They were running now. Not advisable at this elevation but Jake could not keep himself from hurtling headlong toward the lower woods.

"Just trust me…we have to…it's imperative that we…um…we have to get off the mountain before…"

If Jake Berman were a cartoon, he would have, at that moment, skidded to a stop in a cloud of cartoon smoke, his heels digging in as though they were the twin scoops of some massive bulldozer. But, alas, he was beholden to the physical laws of the universe, and when he tried to come to an abrupt halt right then, he instead tripped and tumbled to the hard-pack.

He slammed against a necklace of stones, his shoulder taking most of the impact. He saw stars. He gasped for breath as he scuttled back to his feet. The others were standing behind him now, staring at the lower elevations. Nobody said anything. Jake realized that *they* could hear what *he* was hearing, and *they* knew that *he* knew that *they* knew this was not good.

Backing away from the noise, Jake gaped at the thick wall of long leaf spruce and pines. Below the tree line, the forest roiled with awful noises. Watery, guttural, feral noises that seemed to be slowly rising in volume, as if something unthinkable, unnamable, imponderable, were coming toward them. And farther down, much fainter, and more distant…the keening sound of human screams.

"Ch-ch-change in plans," Jake uttered, his voice barely audible above the rising din.

"What? *What?*" Sarah saw her father backing up the trail, his horrorstricken gaze locked on the woods. She saw him turn and begin to flee up the side of the mountain. He looked like a rabbit being chased by a dog the size of Godzilla. "What's happening? – WHAT'S GOING ON?"

"COME ON!"

"Holy shit," Todd McFetridge marveled under his breath. He had not been able to tear his gaze from the tree line, and he was unfortunate enough now to see the source of Jake Berman's terror burst from the barrier of ancient pines and skeletal birch trees.

Todd turned and charged up the trail, taking the hairpins so fast his backpack tore loose and went flying.

The text had come from the device of one Dr. Herbert "Bud" Henniman, Jake's colleague at the lab, a long-suffering widower and big brain whom Sarah had met at an agonizingly boring staff cocktail reception at the lab last spring. The message was simple enough, brief, even terse –

> **breech in the containment room virus x now in atmosphere save yourselves all is lost all is lost dear God all is lost all is**

– and in spite of the dearth of punctuation, it was loaded with portents. For nearly an hour after it had initially flickered across the smart phone's display, Jake refused to reveal its implications to the others. He was in too big of a hurry to reach the high ground above fourteen thousand feet. Maybe they would be safe there...*maybe*.

The teenagers struggled to keep up with him, every few moments demanding to know what the hell was going on and why was Jake not telling them anything and where the hell were they going and what *were* those freaky things coming up the trail. Jake kept churning toward the higher elevations. Behind them, the results of the virus reaching a level of four-hundred-and thirty-three-parts-per-million in the atmosphere came shambling toward them, the kind of mutations no ordinary nightmare could ever conjure, now closing the distance to about five hundred yards.

"Come on! – COME ON!" Jake called over his shoulder as he awkwardly vaulted across a narrow gap between two sun-bleached, burnished boulders. "Follow the little cairns of stones – see 'em?! – the little piles ahead of us!!"

His chest throbbed, his joints aching with each leaping stride, his oxygen-starved blood cells fizzing painfully within his marrow. The air was so thin, he felt as though his eyeballs might pop out of his skull at any moment. He refused to slow down, though, or yield to the angry, profane complaints coming from the surly teenagers on his heels. He knew the damage that these things – he would now and forever more think of them as *The Infected* – could do to the physical body. Jake had seen it under controlled conditions in the lab.

"HURRY!" He threw a glance over his shoulder. "They can't get to us on the east face!"

This part of the tundra had been affectionately dubbed 'The Boulder Field' in the brochures – a vast, arid, moon-like plain the size of ten football fields strewn haphazardly with gigantic granite monoliths – on which hikers were forced to leap-frog from rugged facet to rugged facet, following the little mounds of pebbles, until they reached the final 'Home Stretch' of trail which led up the sheer face of bone-gray granite to the summit.

Jake saw a lone tent a hundred yards away, its buttercup yellow nylon flapping in the fifty-mile-an-hour gusts. He hurried toward it. The teens labored after him, shouting obscenities. When Jake reached the little crater of a wind-break in which the tent had been pitched, he saw the body lying half way out its exit flap. "Oh Jesus...don't do this," Jake muttered, kneeling.

The stranger had already succumbed to the virus – God only knew how he had contracted it – and now lay in his sweat damp fleece, face-down on the hard-packed earth. He looked to be a man in his mid-forties, maybe younger, it was hard to tell with the black mold of death darkening his features. The dried foam of spittle ringed his lips.

Sarah and Todd knelt behind Jake, silent now with terror, eyes wide, taking it all in. Todd reached down, picked up the man's fallen sunglasses, and began to ask in a quavering voice, "How did this dude – ?"

The dead man's eyes popped open.

Sarah let out an involuntary shriek as the dead man's hand shot out – his extremities already metamorphosing into new, hybrid, nearly unrecognizable body parts – clutching at the air around Todd McFetridge's arm and finally latching onto the teenager's shirt.

The rest happened so quickly, it would never fully register in their memories other than a blur of nails, teeth, tentacles, blood, and screams.

If Jake Berman had not possessed the mental fortitude, the presence of mind, the sheer *resolve* to grab the dead climber's rucksack before fleeing the scene, he and his daughter would have very likely been doomed to meet a similarly grisly fate as poor, tattooed, sub-literate Todd McFetridge. But as it happened, Jake's instinct had kicked in, and he knew instantly that the unfortunate boy was gone – bless his heart – and Jake then realized that he and his daughter had one chance to elude the invading army of The Infected.

They grabbed the pack of climbing gear, the pick-axe and rope-loop of pitons dangling from its base, and they ran as fast as their oxygen deprived legs and lungs would carry them toward the base of the east face. They reached the cliff and began scuttling up the nearly vertical granite wall – the only short cut to the summit available to them – without saying a word to each other.

Sarah went first, Jake close behind her, and for nearly an hour they slowly, excruciatingly, *painfully* inched their way upward a single foothold at a time. Jake knew nothing about technical climbing beyond what he had seen in the movies or in magazines, and his daughter knew even less. Sarah Berman's single exposure to mountaineering had been at age seven when she attended a bar mitzvah during which the kids were invited to make an assault on a portable climbing wall rolled into a Hilton Hotel ballroom to the tune of "Celebration" by Kool and the Gang.

And yet...with the slow onslaught of dark, tattered figures closing in on them from across the boulder field...they *somehow*, in some way, *emulated* real mountain climbing that day without plummeting to their deaths. The wind-gusts tried their best to sweep them off the rock face, and the toe-holds sticking out of the crags grew fewer and more far between. But they managed to reach a ledge around fourteen hundred and fifty feet by the time the sun had vanished behind the spires of the west range, the encroaching dusk flooding the cathedrals of stone with night as dark as a disease.

Without a word, Jake shrugged off his pack and collapsed on the ledge. Sarah collapsed next to him.

Jake called it a bivouac. He remembered the word from a National Geographic special on Edmund Hillary's 1953 climb of Mount Everest — the word literally meaning a temporary camp without cover used by soldiers — which tonight, here, on this cursed stone ledge almost three miles above sea level, was simply father and daughter huddling under a flapping lean-to of nylon fashioned from the dead climber's rucksack, the fabric buffeting so severely in the winds it threatened to take flight every few seconds.

"Explain one thing to me," Sarah said, wrapped in a thin blanket, shivering convulsively. Hugging herself, lying in a fetal position under the trembling canopy, she was freezing and dangerously dehydrated. "If this artificial virus you created is so scary — if it turns people into these slobbering beasts, and you can't control it — why the hell would you make it in the first place?"

Jake stared at his daughter. She was all he really had in the world, all he truly loved. He reached out with a shaking, frostbitten hand and caressed her cheek. He thought of her trust fund, her wealthy upbringing in Royal Oak, the obscene amounts of money that had funneled into his family coffers from assets amassed over a century of political patronage. He thought about the silver spoon *he* had been born with, and his attempt to rebel by getting his PhD and making something of himself. He thought about the arrogance with which he and Hennimann had weaponized the Hanta virus. Now he simply licked his chapped lips and replied, "You know...it seemed like a good idea at the time."

Across from him, Sarah Berman just shook her head and looked down at the parched stone floor of the ledge. She started to muster a snarky, facetious reply, when she heard the noise filtering up through the winds. She turned and poked her head out from under the canopy. "Oh God no," she uttered breathlessly as she gazed over the precipice down at the sheer rock face below.

Jake pushed the tent flap aside, leaned over the ledge, and looked down.

At least half a dozen creatures were scuttling spider-like up the side of the vertical stone face. Crabbing slowly but steadily up the crags, their hooked, talon-like fingers seeking purchase in cracks and cleavages, they appeared to have the adhesive climbing traits of flies or tree frogs. Their faces (or at least the parts of them that would nominally be considered faces), now barely visible in the moonlit darkness, craned menacingly upward toward the ledge three hundred feet above them, their shimmering metallic eyes fixing themselves on the humans.

Neither Jake nor Sarah said another word. They moved quickly, gathering up the negligible equipment strewn across the ledge. They hooked carabiners to their belts, and breathed through dry, cracked sinuses the cold, thin air as hot as jets of flames in their lungs.

They knew what they had to do.

They had one last chance.

***

They made it to the summit right around dawn, the culmination of a single brutal last-ditch attempt to survive. Their fingers bloody from the climb, their lungs heaving and burning from hypoxia, their joints aching, they fell to the floor of the hundred square-foot pinnacle.

In the purple light of dawn, the granite apex looked like an enormous amputated stump, the clouds brushing the crest like strips of gauze. Jake sensed the spectacular panorama of the Rockies all around them – the towers of snow-capped peaks emerging from the night in high-def clarity, a picture of God's handiwork – and he began to cry.

He cried for a life wasted on the haughty conceits of wealth, he cried for his miserable prick of a father and all the fortunes that never once succeeded in bringing one iota of happiness to his troubled clan. He cried and cried until he heard two things: the faint, dry, flinty scraping of dead fingers against stone, the sound coming closer and closer, and the bloodless, whispery breath of his daughter's voice.

"Strangest thing," she said as she huddled next to him, clinging to him, putting her arms around him and hugging him to her trembling skinny form. "I'm feeling like I almost still sort of love you...as my dad...because that's what you'll always be...no matter how much you screw up."

"Love you too, kid," he said, and held her face to his chest, her flesh so cold it burned. "Close your eyes, Sweetheart, I think I hear help coming."

In his last conscious thoughts, the errant notions banging around his traumatized brain, he imagined the light of a helicopter coming up over the crest, a xenon spot aimed down at the summit from some Special Forces Huey chopper roaring in to save them, the prop wash nearly blowing them off the summit. That's what happens with rich people. They always get saved at the last possible instant, always come out of any ordeal smelling like a rose.

Jake heard the skitter of cold fingernails scraping at a nearby precipice.

"I can hear the rescue team," Jake whispered to his daughter. "They're coming to save us, kiddo."

She giggled softly, keeping her face buried in the folds of his jacket. Jake could see the girl's bare hand, now as blue-white as porcelain, forming the thumbs-up gesture.

Smiling, Jake patted her shoulder, ignoring the pain and terror and grief as the first of the dark figures appeared like a ghastly marionette across the summit.

Jake closed his eyes and imagined being rescued and continued comforting his daughter, and he spent his last moments on earth in complete denial...

...because that's what rich people do, and it had always worked for Jake.

But as the original prospectus for the virus x defense contract had cautioned in its small print, '*Past performance is no guarantee of future success.*'

COLLECTED POEMS
Bruce Boston

Bruce Boston is the author of fifty books and chapbooks, including the novels *The Guardener's Tale* and *Stained Glass Rain*. His writing has appeared in hundreds of publications, most visibly in *Asimov's SF*, *Amazing Stories*, *Realms of Fantasy*, *Weird Tales*, *Pedestal*, *Strange Horizons*, *Daily Science Fiction*, *Year's Best Fantasy and Horror* and the *Nebula Awards Showcase*. Boston has received the Bram Stoker Award, a Pushcart Prize, the Asimov's Readers' Award, the Rhysling Award, and the Grand Master Award of the SFPA. For more information, visit bruceboston.com.

SOUL OF A VICTORIAN

Too late, you have signed the deed,
when you hear a wailing in the cellar.
You find her blind and stubborn
as a root, naked, draped in old lace.

As you lift her through the trapdoor
the wind begins to pierce the eaves,
to fill the high and narrow rooms
with the reek of wood's damp rot.

She tells of the graves in the yard:
one cat, three dogs, a fetus.
She speaks of an empty carriage,
the rusty stain on the hall paper.

And while you are listening
you taste the dead hours and grasp
the worms' artless consummation:
you feel time between your fingers.

She is slipping back from you,
down to the dark lampshades,
the chest with the broken hasp,
to photographs of forgotten memory.

(*The Anthology of Speculative Poetry*, 1980)

CURSE OF THE GHOST'S WIFE

To spend the day
sated and insecure,
never knowing where
he stands or when
he could appear
with strange demands
from beyond the veil.

To hear the creaking
boards and realize
her lover's tread
is no different than
the witless sighs
of her haunted house
settling into ruin.

To wait through
the darkening hours
for his milky white
ambulation to solidify
and beckon her to bed,
where he rides her long,
with no mean effort,
into the chiaroscuro
of incipient dawn.

To see him rise up
from their excitation
and try on shapelessness
as shadows take,
to watch him stream
beneath the door
like lathered smoke,
to feel his ectoplasm
dry in strange ineradicable
patterns on her sheets,
to sense the silence
of his ever presence

closing down about her
like a graven sleeve,
to spend the day
sated and insecure,
to wait through
the darkening hours
for his milky white
ambulation to appear.

(*Asimov's SF*, January 1989)

THE HOUSE BROODS OVER US

i.
It was always the house with its crumbling eaves and weathered gables, its turrets and cupolas, its ornate fretwork and blank window eyes. It was the house with its sagging porticos and scattered trellises, the dark green vines trailing up the walls until their leaves turned sere and pale in the sun's heat.

It was always the house with its trenched history and ineradicable stains on the hardwood floors, vivid as birthmarks or faded as old scars.

ii.
I gathered the tools of the draftsman's trade with a serious intent, to learn the craft of the cartographer, to create a detailed map with a detailed legend, extensive and accurate, that would not only chart the limits of the house but give specific definition to its varied elaborations.

I set out to explore its multiple levels and seductive recesses, the shadow and substance of its rectilinear maze.

And you came with me in your wayward fashion, less than innocent and far from knowing, to share my explorations and test the dimensions of the world waiting beyond each wall.

iii.
We discovered hallways that led to nothing and others that turned back upon themselves. We entered rooms that were ordered and others in rank disarray

You sat at a slender desk in a high drawing room that bathed your flesh in films of light. I paced beyond the carpet, dictating imaginary letters to composers and poets and heads of state.

We slept in a Victorian boudoir rich in its mock oriental decadence, the portraits of dead sinners gracing our walls.

When I cut my hand on a splintered balustrade, your lips closed on the single drop of blood that welled in the lines of my palm.

iv.
When you turned back, gathering up the ball of yarn you had cleverly

unwound to mark our distracted passage, I ventured farther to uncover corridors and cul-de-sacs that recalled ones we had visited together, standing rooms and sitting rooms and those stripped bare of all decor.

Was it days or only hours that I wandered before you found me crouched against a wall, unable to speak beyond a thirst that filled my body to its pores?

v.

We have settled in the rooms we inhabit and we do not stray past their boundaries. We stay close by our hearth and our fire beneath a mantel lined with framed images of these same rooms.

Beyond us we can feel the house brooding through days of neglect, the accumulated dust sifting into its bones, the sun shadows and moon shadows crawling across deserted floors, the shame in its solitude as it waits for a step to cut the silence.

(*Vestal Review*, 2003)

ON SPENDING THE NIGHT ALONE IN A HAUNTED HOUSE:
A USER'S GUIDE

1. Avoid eating solid food for six hours before entering. Drink water in sufficient quantities to prevent dehydration. Do not drink wine or other spirits, particularly brandy.

2. Wear no jewelry or metal of any kind. Most of all, no gold. Be forewarned that even the fillings in your teeth can serve as foci for etheric discharges.

3. Cut your hair as short as possible. Wear a thick woolen cap or a wig that can be pulled from the head if grabbed from behind. Choose clothing that fits snugly but does not impede your movement. Leave no openings. Pockets should be zippered (plastic) or buttoned.

4. You may take reading material to pass the time, but avoid works of fiction unless they are of a morally uplifting tone. For illumination, use candles made from beeswax.

5. Carry no weapons since they would be useless and only serve to irritate whatever presences appear.

6. Enter the house at the instant of sunset, as the last rays of failing light touch the doorstep, front or back. Choose a downstairs room with as little furniture as possible. If you explore other rooms, move loudly, cough and shuffle your feet. Make you presence known at all times.

7. If you must sleep, do so sitting up, in the downstairs room you have chosen. Do not remove your clothing or shoes.

8. When strange noises – whispers, mumblings, moans, the rattling of chains – begin to sound, act as if nothing untoward is happening. Do not attempt to transcribe the goings on with cameras or tape recorders. If you must make some record of the proceedings, use a small notebook which can be concealed on your person and a crayon made from beeswax.

9. When the walls begin to undulate, when the ceiling seems as if it is lowering upon you, do not panic. These are illusions and cannot harm you.

10. When the apparitions begin to appear do not attempt to converse,

touch, or hinder the movements of ghostly figures in any way. Do not call out or look at them directly. If they come toward you, move out of the way. If they call your name, do not answer. Particularly avoid responding to dead relatives, dead friends, dead pets and headless horsemen.

11. If slavering beasts surround you, if growls, screams and cries for help rise to an infernal din, if all the creatures from the pits of Hell arise...sprouting scabs and running sores and grotesques pustules, eyes dangling from their sockets, brains spilling down their cheeks, strips of raw flesh trailing from their arms and naked torsos...if all of this reaches a feverish pitch, clasp your hands over your head and pray aloud to the Lord who made you.

12. No matter what you experience, do not attempt to leave before the first rays of the rising sun touch the front or back steps. Flight can be fatal. Most often a heart attack is the cause, but in certain documented cases individuals have been torn limb from limb.

13. When you survive the night intact only to discover that you are paralyzed with fright, your throat so raw that all you can manage is a croaking whisper, your mind overflowing with the horrors that have transpired, then you must wait until they come to get you.

14. When they carry you out, when they slip a straitjacket over your suddenly writhing form, when they force you down upon a metal table and plunge a needle of sleep into your veins and incarcerate you in a padded cell, never admit for a second that you are now as mad as the midnight sun. Don't give them the satisfaction.

15. Yes, these images will lodge forever in the chambers of your mind. Their screams will echo and resound for you without respite. They will fill your waking and sleeping consciousness with horripilating visions from beyond the veil, with cold chills and sizzling flanges of pain that will set you trembling at any hour of the day or night

16. But you can do it! I know you can! All you have to do is follow my instructions to the last bloody letter. You can be the first on your block to spend the night alone in a haunted house!

(*Dark Tales & Light*, Dark Regions Press, 1998)

BONE CHIMES
Chad P. Brown

Chad P. Brown was born in Huntington, WV. Once he outgrew his childhood fears of haunted houses, clowns, and toy monkeys with cymbals (although the latter still creeps him out a little bit), he discovered a dark love for writing and an affinity for macabre and eldritch matters. He is an Affiliate member of the Horror Writers Association and has appeared in such anthologies as *SPIDERS*, *Gothic Blue Book Vol. 2 – Revenge Edition*, *Fifty Shades of Decay*, *Mental Ward: Echoes of the Past*, and *Dark Harvest: A Collection of Dark Tales*. He can be found online at chadpbrown.com.

Tyler flipped the switch.

As the chamber door raised open, he pulled on a pair of rubber gloves and grabbed the long-handled, wire-bristled broom leaning against the wall. He glanced into the cremator. Ashes and bone fragments littered the chamber floor. He let out a sigh and began the tedious but vital task of sweeping up the remains.

Even after so many months of employment, he was careful to adhere to the first rule of cremation.

"Always make sure every part of the deceased is removed from the chamber," Rodney had told him on his first day of employment.

As those words replayed through his mind, he swept firmly so nothing was left behind but gently enough so the recently deceased wasn't scattered into the air. Ashes sometimes fell onto the floor, but they would be swept up later and added to the remains.

Tyler still tried his best to avoid it, though. Something about it seemed disrespectful, even worse than dropping someone's casket as it was loaded into the back of the hearse.

He shoved the broom all the way to the back of the chamber and swept forward.

Tyler let out a gasp, the broom slipping out of his hands and dropping onto the linoleum floor with a whip-like smack.

The skull of the deceased had rolled across the chamber floor, the empty eye sockets glaring up at him as it came to a rest beside the pile of ashes.

In the three years he'd been working at the crematorium, Tyler had never seen a skull survive the cremation fires. Hell, he'd never even heard of such a thing happening before from Rodney, who'd been in this business for almost ten years.

Bone fragments inevitably remained, some of them good-sized chunks. But they were placed in the cremulator, or the "Bone Grinder," as it was known in the trade, and pulverized by rotating blades into a fine dust. Afterwards, they were included with the other ashes in the boxed up remains.

Tyler glanced up at the clock on the wall. Rodney would be back from lunch in a few minutes.

He reached forward with shaky hands and scooped up the skull to examine it closer. There was no crack, chip, or burn mark anywhere; he couldn't even tell it had endured flames as scorching hot as 2,000 degrees. Half-expecting it to shatter like brittle eggshells, he rapped his knuckles on top to test the stability of the bone.

It remained intact.

Tyler glanced at the clock again. He needed to hurry. Rodney would be back any minute.

He pulled out a four-inch wide paint brush from his back pocket and brushed any lingering ash off the skull into the pile of remains, careful to abide by Cremation Rule #1 even while contemplating such a vile and atrocious act.

When he was done, he walked over to his locker. He zipped up the skull inside his backpack after carefully wrapping it in an old sweatshirt he always carried with him.

As he shut his locker door, the stairwell door squeaked open and slammed shut, followed immediately by the thump of approaching footsteps.

Tyler darted back over to the cremation chamber and snatched the broom off the floor.

"I'm back from lunch," Rodney mumbled, strolling over to the time clock.

Tyler nodded and absent-mindedly resumed sweeping up the remains, his mind focused on his grandmother and wind chimes.

***

As a child, Tyler had been fascinated by wind chimes.

He would sit in his grandmother's front porch swing for hours and gaze up at the myriad of wind chimes adorning her house. She'd collected them for years, possessing every kind imaginable: aluminum, bamboo, shell, porcelain, glass, stone...she'd even made a set out of some old spoons and forks.

Tyler would close his eyes and allow the wind chimes' magical music to envelope him, more comforting even than his favorite bedtime blanket.

A gentle breeze would compose an enticing, hypnotic jingle, which would cast a deep spell of sleep over him. The gusting wind of an approaching thunderstorm would conduct a cacophony of clanging chaos, as frightening and exhilarating as a roller coaster ride.

When Tyler was little, his grandmother had taught him how to make wind chimes. She'd shown him everything from choosing the best-sounding materials to fastening them securely enough so they withstood the most violent of winds.

It was a skill and an art form.

But wind chimes also served an important purpose, unknown to everyone who purchased them in any dollar store.

"They guard against evil," his grandmother had told him as she handed him the wind chimes she'd constructed for him. "From the earliest of times, it has always been so. The ancient cultures of Rome, India, and China – they all used them to drive away evil spirits. They believed the tinkling sound of the chimes frightened those evil spirits away."

Tyler had hung the wind chimes his grandmother had given him outside his bedroom window in order to drive Bloody Bones away, the terror which had haunted his dreams at night for weeks. According to his grandmother, Bloody Bones was the name her own grandmother had given to the bogeyman. Parents had always threatened their children that the bogeyman would come and get them if they were bad, carry them off at night to gnaw on their skinned bones. Those parents didn't mean any harm; they just wanted to scare their children so they would be good.

But, as with most stories, there was a truth behind it.

Bloody Bones was real, unconcerned whether children were good or bad. He just wanted to feed on their bones.

To Tyler's surprise, the wind chimes had worked. Bloody Bones never threatened him again.

When he reached adulthood, Tyler decorated the entire exterior of his home with wind chimes as if they were Christmas lights, hanging them on the porch and outside every window as well. Neighbors would often complain about the racket and whisper how he was out of his mind, but Tyler didn't care.

He was protected from the wicked forces in the world.

But, a few weeks ago, Tyler had realized there were some evils even wind chimes couldn't drive away.

***

When Tyler got home that evening, he skipped dinner and headed straight down to the basement to get to work. He carefully unwrapped the old sweatshirt, a sliver of fear digging into the pit of his stomach that the skull had been damaged.

But it was safe.

Setting it aside for the moment, he admired the wind chimes he'd partially constructed. His grandmother would've been proud of the craftsmanship even though he knew she would've disapproved of the human bones he'd used to make them.

The base of the wind chimes was comprised of a sternum and the chimes were made from the humerus, ulna, and radius bones of a right arm. He'd chosen the right arm because the right side had been associated with warding off evil from the earliest of times. Two clavicle bones completed the chimes. He'd joined the bones to the sternum with thin nylon cord just as his grandmother had taught him so many years ago.

Now that he'd acquired a skull, Tyler could complete his project.

In a perfect world, the skull would've come from the same corpse which had provided the other bones. But that hadn't been possible. His grandmother had died from a tragic accident, her head violently bashed in.

No one had been aware that his grandmother had been a practitioner of Southern Appalachian folk magic. Power resided in her bones, which Tyler needed to drive away the evil threatening him, even if her shattered skull was useless.

He'd persevered though, patiently waiting for a replacement to present itself to him.

As Tyler worked on attaching the skull to the sternum, the voice began to speak to him again. It taunted him with how he wouldn't stop it from killing again.

When he'd first conceived of the idea of constructing wind chimes out of human bones, Tyler was positive he was going insane. That the thought had even crossed his mind revolted him. But it made sense the more he deliberated it. He could sense the evil threatening him was ancient and powerful. In order to drive it away, he needed magic just as primordial and potent.

Tyler finished attaching the sternum to the base of the skull and began the final step of tying nylon cord to the top of the skull from which to hang the chimes.

The voice continued to mock him, growing louder and more persistent. Tyler squeezed his eyes shut and shook his head. He couldn't allow himself to surrender to the voice and abandon his task.

A couple of minutes later, he held the completed work inches from his face.

"Bone chimes," he said with pride and confidence. "You will protect me."

He rocked his hand back and forth. The bones clanged together, producing a chilling but satisfying sound that brought a smile to his face.

The evil had been silenced.

***

For the first few nights, Tyler could barely sleep because of the clanking of the bone chimes outside his bedroom window. He would hide his head under the pillow or play music on his iPod in an effort to drown out the eerie sounds.

Nothing worked.

But he considered the lack of sleep a fair trade for driving away the evil.

Somehow, though, he grew accustomed to the bone chimes. Although he still couldn't understand it, he found comfort in them, their uncanny sounds enticing him to sleep with their twisted, macabre lullaby.

A couple of weeks later, however, the evil broke its silence.

Tyler had just loaded a corpse into the cremator when he felt a cold chill. Within seconds, he was shivering and blowing on his hands to get them warm.

"What's wrong with you?" Rodney asked when he noticed how Tyler was acting.

"It's freezing in here." Tyler's teeth chattered with each enunciated syllable.

Rodney threw him a skeptical look. "You're joking, right? That thing throws off heat ten times hotter than any oven."

Rodney was right. The fires of the cremator always kept the room unbearably hot. Usually, Tyler was red-faced and dripping sweat.

But right this second, he felt like he'd been shoved inside of a morgue freezer.

"Well, I'm freezing to death," Tyler reiterated. At the mention of death, icy fingers wrapped around his spine causing him to shudder.

He walked over to his locker and put on the old sweatshirt he kept in his backpack. As he pulled it over his head, he caught a glimpse of Rodney shaking his head at him. Tyler closed the locker door and headed back over to the cremator.

He came to a sudden halt halfway across the room when he heard a bizarre noise. Spinning slowly around in a circle, he tried to locate the source of the sound. But all he found was Rodney staring at him even stranger than before.

"Are you alright?" Rodney asked him.

"Do you hear that noise?"

Rodney listened for a moment. "All I hear are the cremation fires."

Tyler shook his head. "No, it isn't that. This sounds like—"

He stopped in mid-sentence when he recognized the peculiar clanging of the bone chimes reverberating off the walls. His eyes darted frantically around the room as the sound of the bone chimes grew louder. The room began to spin. Beads of sweat formed on his brow. His eyes took on a distant, hazy look and his face lost all color.

"Hey, come and sit down." Rodney took Tyler by the arm and led him over to a chair on the other side of the room.

As Tyler sat down, the clanking of the bone chimes transformed into distinct words, the voice sounding like bones pulverized in the all too familiar Bone Grinder.

IT'S COMING AND IT WILL TAKE YOU.

The coppery taste of blood coated his tongue. Tyler gagged, on the verge of puking. Rodney rushed over to the corner of the room and brought back a garbage can, placing it in front of his friend.

Suddenly, the sound of the bone chimes ceased along with the chills, nausea, and shakes plaguing Tyler, which had made him feel like an addict needing a fix.

"I'm going to call an ambulance." Rodney dug into his pocket for his cell phone.

Tyler grabbed his arm, stopping him. "No, don't. I'm okay now."

After a moment, the worried look on Rodney's face gradually dissipated into relief. "You do look a little better. You had me worried for a minute."

"I think I'm coming down with the flu or something," Tyler lied. "Maybe I should just cut out early and head home."

"You sure?" The concerned look on Rodney's face returned. "I don't think you should be driving. Maybe I'd better give you a ride home."

"No, I'm fine."

The last thing Tyler wanted was to take the chance of Rodney discovering the bone chimes hanging outside his bedroom window.

Rodney finally agreed. "Alright. But you call me and let me know you got home safe, alright?"

Tyler nodded his head as he slowly rose to his feet. "I will."

"Okay," Rodney said. "Take the rest of the day and get better, man."

***

Tyler sat on the edge of his bed, staring out the bedroom window in confusion. The wind was blowing, evidenced by the shrill howling and the swaying tree branches scratching violently against the window like some night terror trying to break in.

The bone chimes, however, were motionless and silent.

Tyler grew frightened, unsure of what it meant. The magic of the bone chimes had been powerful enough to drive the evil away. He hadn't heard the voice in weeks. But earlier, they'd warned him something was coming to get him. To his dismay, they now refused to elaborate on or even reiterate the warning.

He was starting to doubt that the bone chimes had spoken to him earlier at work. It didn't, after all, make sense how he'd heard them miles away from his home or why they were silent now.

But maybe the evil was back, using deception to get to him.

The doorbell rang, startling him and shaking him out of his thoughts.

Tyler tore his eyes away from the bedroom window and glanced at the clock on his nightstand. It was almost seven o'clock. He'd been staring at the bone chimes for more than four hours and hadn't even realized it.

As he pondered what kind of hold the bone chimes had on him, more powerful than any lover's embrace, he heard a loud and persistent knock.

Tyler crept down the stairs and cautiously approached the front door, wondering who in the hell it could be. No one ever came to visit him, and it was too late for a wandering salesman or pamphlet-pushing evangelist.

He opened the door only to discover no one was there.

He glanced around in confusion. There were no cars in the driveway other than his own Ford Taurus.

It must be some damn kids pulling a prank, he thought as he stepped back inside and slammed the door.

Tyler turned to go back upstairs but stopped when he heard a pounding at the back door. Muttering to himself and determined to catch the little brats in the act, he strode towards the back of the house. He stepped into the kitchen and froze, spotting a large shadow silhouetted in the frosted glass of the doorway, which was definitely no child.

IT'S HERE.

Tyler jumped when he heard the chilling, grinding voice of the bone chimes. The doorknob jiggled incessantly back and forth, causing him to jump again.

IT'S COMING FOR YOU.

Tyler glimpsed around the kitchen for something to use as a weapon. He spotted the pipe wrench still sitting on the counter from when he'd worked on the sink last weekend. He tiptoed over and snatched it.

It wasn't much, but he hoped it would be enough to bash in the head of whatever was coming for him.

He glanced at the door. The looming shadow remained.

KILL THE EVIL.

Tyler nodded his head, agreeing wholeheartedly with the bone chimes' rational suggestion. He raised the pipe wrench above his head and flung open the door.

"Whoa, buddy! It's only me!"

"Rodney?" Tyler stared at his friend in shock. "What are you doing here?"

Rodney let out a sigh of relief as Tyler lowered the pipe wrench. "I came by to check on how you were doing. You never called to let me know you made it home."

Tyler had been so preoccupied with the bone chimes that he'd forgotten about promising Rodney to let him know he was alright. "Sorry, it slipped my mind."

"That's okay. There was no answer at the front door, so I came around back."

Tyler grew suspicious. "Where's your truck at? I didn't see it in the driveway."

"I parked up the street. I don't see too great at night and I wasn't sure which house was yours. I walked up and down this block until I spotted your car in the driveway."

Tyler accepted his friend's explanation. During the past few years they'd known each other, Rodney had only been over to his house a couple of times, and that was to drop Tyler off after they'd gone out for a couple of beers after work.

Rodney looked Tyler up and down, trying to determine if his friend felt any better. "How you feeling?"

"Alright," Tyler answered. If anything, he felt like he was losing his mind more than ever.

"Well, at least you look better." Rodney's eyes drifted down to the pipe wrench still in Tyler's hand. "Scared me for a minute with that thing. Thought for sure you were going to clobber me."

"Sorry, I thought you were somebody trying to break in." Tyler turned and laid the wrench down on the kitchen table.

"When there was no answer back here, I started getting worried since your car was parked out front. I thought you might be in here half-dead or something."

An awkward silence followed. As the seconds ticked by, Rodney rocked back and forth on his heels, uncomfortably waiting to be invited inside.

Tyler didn't notice, his thoughts lingering on the bone chimes. Maybe he was going crazy, imagining the voice. The atrocity of his actions in constructing the bone chimes smacked him in the face like an offended lover. He vowed to take them down and to destroy the abhorrent creation that he'd brought into his house.

"Well, I just wanted to check on you," Rodney said when it became apparent Tyler wasn't going to ask him inside.

Tyler snapped back to the present, finally noticing the offended look in

Rodney's eyes, who'd drove all the way over to check on him. The least he could do was invite him in. "I'm sorry, man. You want to come in for a beer?"

Rodney glanced at his watch. "Sure, a beer would be great."

Tyler stepped aside and let his friend inside. He walked over and opened the fridge, glancing at the shelves. "All I've got is light beer. Is that alright?"

"That'll be fine."

Tyler grabbed two beers and shut the fridge. He turned to hand one to Rodney, catching sight of the empty kitchen table.

He watched in helpless terror as the pipe wrench came down and cracked his head.

***

Rodney crept up the stairs.

Tyler was still in the kitchen, his smashed-in head spewing forth a stream of blood onto the tan linoleum floor. Rodney had hated to kill his friend, but it had been necessary.

He cracked open the bedroom door and peeked inside. On the far side of the room, the bone chimes hung outside the window. He pushed the door open and walked over to them, unable to pull his awe-filled eyes away from their enticing pull.

Earlier, when he'd made his way around to the back of the house, he'd spotted the bone chimes hanging outside the upstairs window. At first, he'd thought he was hallucinating. Now, standing only a couple of feet away from them, he still couldn't believe they were real.

For weeks, he'd thought he was going insane. The unrelenting voice speaking to him, insisting the evil must be stopped.

He'd been convinced it had all been in his head.

But it had led him here and to the abomination inside this house.

Rodney raised the window and eagerly snatched the bone chimes. He held them up and shook them. A brief shudder passed through him as the bones clanked together.

"Will you come home with me," he whispered, "and protect me from evil?"

The bone chimes spoke.

YES, WE WILL.

THE BUTTERFLY GARDENER
Tara Cleves

Tara Cleves is a 30-year resident of the Sunshine State. Though she loves the sun, the Florida moon equally enchants her. Librarian by day, Tara spends her evenings figuring out what to watch now that *True Blood* is over, and writing fiction. On weekends, she visits sea turtles in rehab, and she spends sunny afternoons and moonlit evenings in her butterfly garden or at the beach for sea turtle releases. Her published works include a dreary romantic poem some years ago, a novel *The Guardian of Baine Manor*, a short story *The B&B Owner* published by Burial Day Books, and now, *The Butterfly Gardener* for this year's *Gothic Blue Book: The Folklore Edition*.

I had no idea what I was doing wrong. I dug holes, I planted plants, I watered every day, and sure, the sun shone and things grew and things bloomed. But never, ever did a butterfly *once* visit my garden.

That was the promise at the butterfly gardening workshop—if you plant it, they will come. I giggled when the workshop gal said that, recalling the movie *Field of Dreams*—if you build it, he will come. I imagined butterflies wielding tiny baseball bats while caterpillars flung poop from their back ends like baseballs.

No, not poop.

Frass.

I learned that word at the workshop. Caterpillars poop frass. Rhymes with, well, the *other* word for back end, and it smells like grass. I know this because, when I was little, I once raised a caterpillar on a cabbage leaf. I so hoped it would become a butterfly, but like my mother warned me, it pupated and emerged as a moth.

I learned those words at the workshop, too.

Pupate.

Emerge.

And a butterfly does not make a cocoon. A moth makes a cocoon. A butterfly makes a...

Chrysalis.

When I first said the word chrysalis, it was like fresh shaved ice on my tongue. And as beautiful as the word is to hear and say, the monarch butterfly chrysalis is most beautiful to see—a jade green almond with specks of gold. In generic descriptions of a monarch's pupal stage, that phrase comes up—jade green with specks of gold. At the workshop, we beheld a monarch chrysalis. It truly was jade green and flecked with gold. I wanted jewelry made of that chrysalis, strung like beads around my neck while I spun in a flowery dress. I wanted butterflies in my hair, on my shoulders, flitting like heaven all around me...

Instead, I was hot and thirsty. Dirt caked my knees and hair, sweat soaked my tank top, and not one butterfly had visited in the weeks I'd had my garden. I had planted great plants, too: Passion vine and dill, globes of red pentas, cute bachelor's buttons, and a sure-fire section of milkweed for the migratory monarchs. I loved the monarchs best. Long-lived butterflies which flew cross-country, believed to be the souls of the dead in Mexican tradition.

Yet, nothing came. Not butterflies anyway. What I had was a right-proper lizard and ant garden. Still, I was out there yet again, planting firebush this time, hoping the blooms would finally attract butterflies. Maybe if I added citrus for the swallowtails...a lime tree here, a lemon tree there...

Ugh. Who was I kidding?

I threw down my shovel and gardening gloves, mustering a curse as I stomped toward the house. Once inside, I kicked the kitchen table for good measure only to squeak at the pain that shot through my toe. To top it off, the vase I had bought at the butterfly garden gift shop tipped and rolled off the table, crashing into pieces on the floor.

I wanted to cry. I nearly did cry, too, when my house phone rang me to distraction. Wiping my face with a grimy hand, I hobbled around pieces of vase to the phone. I must have sounded shaken when I answered, because the first words from my mother on the other end were, "Honey, you all right?"

"Yes, yes, I'm fine," I assured her, re-doing my pony-tail as I cradled the phone on my shoulder. While I relayed my garden frustrations to her, I scrounged for a glass of water. The gulping gave me hiccups, so I told her I'd call her later, that I loved her, and hung up the phone.

Just in time, too. I could tell she cared less about the garden, and really wanted news about my job hunt, a hunt she was compelled to lead. Her latest find was a management position at a cemetery office. "You have to think outside the box, dear," she had said, patting my hand over another very tiring lunch about my lack of work of late. "They make good money, like any other office management job," she assured me while I stared at the dead shrimp on my salad. When I joked that the little fellas could use good deathcare services, she swatted my hand in exasperation. Still, she insisted I take the business card and, like a good daughter, I told her I would call and apply.

But I did not call.

I did not apply.

Instead, I spent another forty dollars on butterfly plants and another weekday in my yard instead of out looking for work. And look where that got me—a stubbed toe, a broken vase and a near breakdown into tears, tears that would shed if I stood idle a moment longer. I shook my head clear and grabbed the broom, sweeping the broken vase into a pile. It was a pretty vase, white with cobalt blue glass butterflies. As I swept, the pieces slid along the floor as if they were flying, their jeweled wings glinting in the kitchen window light…

Jeweled wings.

Those words caught in my mind—had I heard them somewhere or made up the phrase some time ago? No, I'd *seen* the phrase…I leaned on the broom, squinting my eyes in recollection. *Ah!* I dropped the broom in a mad dash for my purse. Tearing through my wallet, I found it—a card—the business card my mother gave me. The card for the cemetery.

Yes, there were the words, black-on-white, with a butterfly logo—

The Jeweled Wing Gardens and Memorial Park.

***

As I pulled into the parking lot of Jeweled Wing Gardens and Memorial Park, ten butterflies flew past my car. *Ten.* Maybe more. White ones flitting along the grass and orange-and-silver beauties twirling like acrobats. A lemon-yellow guy bobbled past my skirt as I followed a brick sidewalk toward a small cottage marked 'Office.' On my approach, an overwhelming need to work in this place gripped my chest. Maybe it was weeks of no job. Maybe it was my dwindling bank account and the tone in my mother's voice of late.

Maybe it was the butterflies.

One more flitted past my face before I reached the door of the office, a fine zebra-striped darter. He hovered on the door handle, and as I reached for the knob, I whispered, "Go to my garden, *go*! I have what you need…"

The door creaked open, sending the long-winged fellow flying. A woman peered out at me—small, slim, with knotted hair and a face that masked her real age. "It's possible you have what we need," she stated, unsmiling.

"We shall see." I blushed, waving a little. She gestured me inside.

"Miss Monroe, I presume?"

I nodded, taking in the sparse quaintness of the place. "Please, call me Haddy," I replied. Yes, plain ol' Haddy. Nothing like my surname movie star namesake, though I could pass for Marilyn if I did my hair and lips just so.

The woman gestured me toward a cane-back chair. I complied, crossing my ankles and feeling like, well, like a girl on her first job interview. Truly, it was the third interview in my life. And though I was well past girlhood, it was my first at a cemetery—how do the living conduct themselves anyway when they want in on a cemetery?

The slim little woman clacked across the wooden floor to another door, rapping hard before opening it. I heard her call into the room, "Miss Monroe here to see you, sir."

Sir?

Okay, a gentleman was my could-be boss. Why had I figured on a female? I knew why. It was his name. Darcy. Darcy Seymour. It conjured images of old English novels and Jane Seymour, the actress I'd loved since her movie role in *Somewhere In Time*. Christopher Reeve was in it too, yearning for a woman born and died long before his time...

"Miss Monroe? *Miss Monroe?*"

The small woman was bent toward me.

"Oh! So sorry," I said, rousing from my dreamy reverie.

The woman stood up straight, folding her arms. "Mr. Seymour will see you now."

I stood, and as I walked toward the man's office, I felt that clinch again in my chest, like I would shatter if I didn't get this job. I hadn't interviewed in forever, and I wasn't sure if I should shake hands or immediately take a seat, or beg for work on my knees, *Oh, God, this was it...*

***

When I stepped into Darcy Seymour's office, my greeting died on my lips. A smell like flowers and alcohol tinged the air, and what I could see of the man was encased in white. White lab coat. White latex gloves. White mask and head gear like a surgeon's garb.

He peered at me through black framed eyeglasses and nodded to a chair by his desk. I sat, but his actions were mesmerizing, like a stage magician. He stood at a counter along one wall, his back to me, so staring was easy. He reached for a glass jar then upward into a cabinet for a wooden box with a clear glass lid, laying it open on the counter. He rooted through a drawer, muttering, then slammed it shut and pulled open another drawer. His gloved hand emerged with tweezers, at which point he unscrewed the jar lid and jammed the tweezers inside the jar. I heard clicking against the glass, then slowly, slowly, his hand emerged...

Dangling from the tweezers, stiff and still, was a butterfly of such size and color that I gasped.

Mr. Seymour read my gasp as a compliment, responding, "Gorgeous, isn't she?" Then he lay the inert insect into the wooden box. He stood back, waggling his fingers around more drawers, and pulled one open; pins this time, long, thin pins in a plastic container.

I could not see what he was doing, but I knew. His arm reached for a pin then disappeared into his hunch over the box. Seven, eight times— reach and pin, reach and pin.

Then with both hands, he closed the glass lid and caressed it like he was smoothing the wrinkles on a made bed. He stepped back, his hands on his hips in pride. "My first swallowtail butterfly," he announced. "Would you like to see?" His eyes were wide and crinkled from the grin behind his mask.

I shook my head *No...no...*and hoped my reticence wouldn't cost me the job interview.

He shrugged, then started peeling off his lab garb. Once he was down to his khakis and sweater vest, he sat across from me and shuffled papers on his desk. I recognized my job application and waited for him to quit perusing it and actually address me. His eyeglasses were huge on his face— thick and round, like bug eyes. His mouth opened and closed and he nodded his head like he was reading through bifocal lenses.

"How do you kill them?"

He flicked his stare from the paper to me. "Come again...?"

"The butterflies," I gestured at the jars on the counter. "how do you kill them?"

"I enclose them in a jar with a cotton ball soaked in rubbing alcohol or I freeze them." He went back to reading my application.

"How long does it take them to die?"

"A few hours."

"Then you pin them?"

"Yes. While they are still pliable."

"How long do they hold their color after they die?"

"Forever, Miss Monroe." He laid down the paper. "You sure you don't want to see the one I just pinned?"

I shook my head hard. "*No. No.*"

Behind the man, a huge picture window framed the cemetery gardens. A dozen or so butterflies lit on headstones and meandered in the air.

I pointed. "You ever capture those guys?"

He turned to the window. "Sometimes. Or, I raise them from caterpillars. They're perfect right when they start flitting inside the jar—"

I got up. "I have to go."

He twirled in his chair to face me. "What?"

I grabbed my application from his fist and exited Darcy Seymour's office.

***

I'd never heard of such a thing. I drove and mentally inventoried my stock of lidded glass jars. Did I have rubbing alcohol? I swerved into a pharmacy parking lot and bought two large bottles of the stuff. My cell phone rang. *Ugh,* my mother, no doubt wondering about my job interview. I ignored the call and continued on to my next stop—a chain toy-store a mile up the highway. Once inside, I weaved past baby strollers and shopping carts packed with toddlers, pushed by parents babbling like lawyers to demanding clients. Two rows ahead a sign said 'Science and Nature.' *Bingo!* I grabbed what I sought and headed for check-out.

When I got home, I spread my loot on the kitchen table. I also grabbed cotton balls and every lidded jar in my cabinets. I sat and carefully weighed the task before me, starting with the box from the toy store:

Flit-n-Fly Butterfly Hatching Kit.

Then I devoured the instructions for sending in my 'caterpillar voucher' and estimated the time for five Painted Lady butterfly larvae to arrive at my house, pupate and emerge as butterflies. I picked up my other toy store purchase: a wooden-handled butterfly net. It was the real deal, no plastic kid's version with fake bugs in its nylon netting. I swung it, watching it flail and drift in the air. *I'll get you suckers,* I thought. *No escape now.*

I checked the time. Six o'clock. Plenty of time to eat and do my next phase of research before bed.

After dinner, I curled up on the living room sofa with a steaming cup of tea and my laptop. Jeweled Wing Gardens and Memorial Park had a beautiful website. The music and voice-over were cheesy, but the photographs were a delight. Butterfly graphics flit across the text. *Hm, nice touch,* I thought. *Die surrounded by insects that hold their color longer than you will after death.* Pretty website, but not what I needed.

I clicked more around the web, searching the street address, and *yes!* A recent, aerial view of the property popped into view. The office building. The parking lot. The surrounding trees and lawn. I scoured the area, following the cemetery's interior pathways to its remotest corner with the fewest trees, *and the most sun...*I got excited. *That's the place!* I caressed the screen. *That's where I'll be at dawn.*

***

It was still dark when I pulled into the cemetery car lot. A chill shook me and I grabbed my scarf along with my butterfly net. I had a bucket, too,

44

with a lid to keep my jewels from escaping. I walked through the cover of early dark along the paths till I found my private spot of lawn and gravestones. I paused in the surrounding tree line, spread my scarf on the ground, sat down—and waited.

Within the half-hour, birds chirped, and shaded dawn gave way to bright, filtered light. I smacked at gnats around my face, the dew at my feet drying out in the warming air. The morning grew brighter. The cemetery's hazy gardenscape soon burst into daylight greens and blooms of butterfly plants. Some I recognized, others were new to me. I basked in the scene, hushed, expectant. Something flew past me...just a dragonfly, then a bee...and one yellow butterfly.

It was a sulphur. Cloudless? Orange-barred? *Hard to tell, so flighty.*

I stood, my net in hand. The yellow jewel fluttered along the lawn, alighting on a bloom the color of its wings. I walked toward it, not fast, not slow, a steady glide and, *whoosh.* In my net it went, twisting the handle to seal the creature's escape. *Like a fly on a frog's tongue,* I thought merrily. The bug grappled inside the net then settled. I transported it back to my spot in the trees, tapped it into the bucket, and slid the lid in place. I could hear flutters and bumps, then it went quiet. When I turned toward the clearing, half a dozen butterflies were tangling in the sunny air. I bounded toward them, scooping two in one swipe. They had orange-silver markings, *wow,* the Gulf Fritillary. Out of nowhere zoomed a big, black fellow with yellow lace along its hindwings. Pipevine swallowtail, *yes.* I scooped and swiped and *swooshed* till the lunchtime sun made my belly growl.

By noon, eighteen butterflies sat in my bucket. Amazing they didn't fly free every time I made a deposit. But I managed—not one lost, not one mangled—and I gathered a scarf, net and bucket for the walk to the car.

"Excuse me, ma'am."

I turned toward the voice. A man in shorts and a work shirt approached. His cap bore the cemetery's logo—a black-and-white hand-drawn butterfly. I said an immediate *Hello,* and then...

"Please, sir, I'm looking for my mother's plot. My dad is meeting me, then we are headed to the lake." I held up the net and bucket. "I'm taking him fishing."

The man squinted at my net. "Fishing, huh?"

"Yes, it's easier for him with this since his stroke." *Please, please, stay still. He'll hear your wings.* I coughed. "Anyway, the Monarch Garden, is it this way?" I nodded toward the car lot, knowing the garden was in the same direction.

The man's face softened. He still eyed my net and bucket, but he nodded. "Sure, straight ahead. Net fishing, with that thing, damn if I ever heard of it." Then he walked away.

And I caught a breath, and ran to my car.

***

I'd no idea what I was doing. Yet, there were eighteen glass jars on my kitchen table, each one containing an alcohol-soaked cotton ball and a cemetery butterfly. I was still in my day's T-shirt and skirt, squatting by the jars as wings fluttered or slowly opened and closed. *A few hours to die. Pin them while they are pliable.* I could do that. I'd bought pins, too, at the quilt shop by my mother's house.

I checked my stove clock. Plenty of time before sundown. I had other things to do, chores, errands, *job hunting*...But I stayed by the table. Hour after hour, walking around the jars, watching, taking in the color and movement till my back and knees hurt from kneeling and standing. Then, at quarter-till-six, all at the same time...

Three butterflies went completely still.

Tweezers, tweezers, where...I grabbed them from the kitchen counter, along with a cookie sheet covered with parchment paper. First jar opened, first butterfly on the sheet. The next two jewels, *oops, damn,* nearly dropped the third one. It was gorgeous—a malachite, I couldn't believe it. Like green stained glass. Four more insects went still, and by twilight, seventeen butterflies were spread across two cookie sheets. Some lay open, some were closed flat, but all were pliable, their wings moving if I squeezed the thorax. I grabbed the pins and the butterfly sheets.

And headed toward the garden.

***

"Mrs. Monroe? Can you answer some questions?"

Candace Monroe, sixty-one years old, dressed in a bird's egg blue skirt suit, a matching bag, and nurse's shoes for her bunions, sat on a stone bench beside her daughter's butterfly garden. Two feet from her lay her daughter's body, covered in a coroner's tarp.

"I already did." She pointed to a police officer by the fence. "Now, please, leave me alone." The officer at her side nodded, and as bid, left the woman alone.

Candace stared at the tarp. Strewn in the grass were cookie sheets and some sort of slick, white paper. There was also a thirty-foot orange cord running through the yard, plugged into a standing electric fan aimed at the garden. She eyed the cord, pausing at the frayed section, one of many frays, brushing against the broken sprinkler head. Water dribbled from the sprinkler, adding to the mud puddle in the wet grass. Haddy's father had given her that cord, said she needed practical things around the house. Candace had dearly loved her husband, through his first stroke, then his second, but the man would never throw anything away, even if it was broken to the point of dangerous. Candace stared at the cord. *Just like her father.*

She looked at the garden. It was full of blooms, lush green leaves and vines. *The butterflies do look pretty,* she thought. *Even the pin heads match the color of the wings. So Haddy.* Candace stood and stepped to the garden's edge. She touched a butterfly, a yellow one with vertical orange bars, like pastel smudges. Splayed on a flame vine, its snout pinned against a bright orange bloom. Stiff. Still.

Too still.

Candace pondered the perched and pinned butterflies, looking more like prisoners than free-flying guests. She reached into her purse, retrieving the jar she'd found on her daughter's kitchen table. Inside was a butterfly, a monarch. The two days since it died, its wings had stiffened in a near-open position. She unscrewed the jar's lid and slowly shook the butterfly into her palm. Then she leaned down to the spilt box of quilting pins at the garden's border. *Two should do it.* Grasping a milkweed plant, she stabbed the insect through its neck and thorax, onto a leaf of the plant. Milky substance from the plant wet her fingers. The butterfly loped to one side but stayed put. She eyed the fan, then faced the monarch. She inhaled deep the scent of the blooms, and blew.

PARCEL POST
M. Frank Darbe

M. Frank Darbe has been a resident of California since 1970. He likes writing fiction and poetry, hiking, travel, camping, reading, politics, model railroading, war-gaming (with painted miniatures), coffee, long conversations by candlelight, and an occasional glass of fine Tequila. Darbe has a Masters of Fine Arts in Creative Writing from National University. Over the years, he has published six short stories in small markets and 13 poems in *99 New Poems: A Contemporary Anthology* (2010).

Andrew Timberline stepped down onto the running board of his mail truck, pulled his handkerchief from his pocket, wiped the sweat from his face, and then chanted. "Neither rain nor snow nor heat my ass." Whoever wrote that little ditty never visited Louisiana in the summer of 1913. Nine in the morning and already hot as the fires of hell, and wet as the bottom of the bayou, with the unmoving air full of sweat flies and noseeums.

He twisted his head around, and scanned the front of the white-walled convent that sprawled along the side of the road behind an iron fence. He'd lived all his life in New Orleans' Ninth Ward and had more than a passing acquaintance with the Ursuline Nuns, though he had never been inside the iron fence that marked the borders of their domain. They had always been holy hell on boys with unruly mouths. He doubted time had gentled them. "Best keep my profane mouth quiet."

He grabbed his leather mailbag from the back of the truck and followed the walkway through the open gate into the shadows of the convent. Two nuns dressed in habits of black tunic, white caps, and black veils jerked weeds from the sinful soil while whisperings acts of contrition.

Beyond the garden, beyond a long series of brick arches, in an open area at the front of the convent, an older nun counted her rosary with grim discipline, her pale face was a near seamless continuation of the white cap that surrounded it.

She dropped her beads and frowned, "You are late," and then added "Mr." as a question.

He nodded and answered, "Andrew Timberline. You've got packages for the post?" She was wrong, of course, though he wasn't a man to argue with a nun.

"Follow me." She glided with singular grace as if she floated above the ground by the power of God, setting a pace that stretched Andrew's long legs. She led him around the side of the convent in the shadows of a hedge of camellias, surrounded by the high fey laughter of young girls from the convent school. Their disembodied voices faded as they turned a corner and caught sight of an old cemetery full of white crypts built above the ground as was the custom in older, lower areas of New Orleans.

"Where are the packages?" He asked, preferring the pleasant sound of the conversation of the living to the quiet neighborhoods of the dead.

"Inside," she said as she pulled a largish key from somewhere in her habit and unlocked an oak door. A narrow passage through the convent's thick walls opened into a large vaulted space. Bands of light angled down from tiny, clerestory windows set high in the walls that illuminated a worn, red tile floor, and a large table with a concave surface of the type used to wash the dead before burial. A faint sweet smell of old death tainted the air. Shelves lined the walls, though he could not tell what, if anything, occupied the shelves. At the far end, near another door leading deeper into the convent, a different sister sat in the shadows at a battered desk.

"Sister Angeline will assist you." She waved at the desk and then glided away.

Sister Angeline sat with a ledger open, dipped her quill in an open inkstand, tapped the excess ink away, and wrote a line. When she finished, she read the words in silence, searching, he thought, for some error that she would need to scratch out and rewrite. She nodded, satisfied, and picked up a small leather rag to clean the quill.

"Mr. Timberline?" She looked up into his face.

How can anyone so old remain alive? Perhaps sinew once existed beneath her skin, but time's merciless river long ago eroded the flesh from beneath, leaving the skin as a winding sheet for the bones.

"Ah, that's me."

"Good. The packages are there." She turned her ancient face and pointed her nose at the people in the shadows behind her desk. "You will find everything in order."

Two individuals sat on the bench wearing identical hooded cloaks, hoods pulled up so that shadows obscured their faces. Nuns there to help an elder sister in menial tasks, he thought, until they turned their faces so that they caught the light. "Those are children, sister."

"Yes." She took her pen and checked the tip to see if it needed sharpening.

"I was directed to pick up two packages, one forty-eight pounds, and the other forty-seven and a half.

"We weighed them. It is all correct."

"People are not parcels."

She pushed her chair back and stood. Andrew looked up into the most remarkable dark eyes, bright and sharp as needles, less the eyes of an ancient nun than of some mad infant. He took a step back.

"We read news reports in this convent, Mr. Timberline. Parcel Post guarantees delivery of all packages within the specified weight limit, even children. Several have been mailed and delivered to family members. The post office supervises them to their ultimate destination."

"Yes ma'am, that has happened."

"And it will happen today again." She looked down her nose at him. "You do understand?"

Andrew shook his head, sighed. "Yes, ma'am." There was no arguing with nuns.

"Deliver them to 2805 Indian Hill Road, St. Bernard Parish, to a Madeline Duchene. An address label with fifty-seven cents in postage is tied to each of their cloaks." She stopped and removed something from a desk drawer. "You will need this." She held out an old iron key.

"That's a long drive." He shook his head. "Take all day. How am I supposed to feed them?"

"You are not to feed them, Mr. Timberline."

"But we are hungry." The girls whispered in high soft voices.

Sister Angeline turned to glare at them. "You have food in your bags. They hold all you are allowed to eat. I expect you to act like young ladies. Do not wolf your food. Take small bites, and you can make it last all day." She turned back. "Best hurry, Mr. Timberline. The girls must be delivered to their mother before dark."

Sister Angeline sat, dipped her quill in the inkstand, and returned to her ledger.

He rounded the desk and the girls rose to meet him. They wore the perfect children's faces, round, pale, with eyes a size and a half too large for their heads and full red lips. "I am Mr. Timberline," he said.

"Pleased to meet you." They smiled, nodded, and curtsied, almost as if they had but one brain to command both bodies.

They followed him out of the chapel mortuary and around the convent to the truck. Busy wondering where he would put the two, he did not realize until he stood at the back of the truck looking in that he had not bothered to ask their names.

"What should I call you?"

"Mary," one said.

"Jane," the other followed.

He glanced over his shoulder. "Mary and Jane Duchene. The rhyming twins." He laughed at his joke.

"Not Duchene," Mary frowned. "The last name is Doe."

Jane continued, "After our father, John Doe."

There was that other thing the Convent was known for, a hospital for wayward women, but it was none of his business upon which side of the blanket these girls were made. A Postman delivered the mail.

He pointed into the back of the mail truck with its space down below for bags and a caged area above for packages. "This won't hold a man," he smiled at the girls who looked back at him with huge soft eyes, "but a couple of young girls should have all the room they need."

Andrew picked each of them up and placed them into the back of his truck, and noticed an odd smell, sweet, like the old death stink in the mortuary. "A pleasant drive in the hot Louisiana sun will do you good."

***

Hours later, while Andrew sat next to the Mississippi, eating his sandwich and a cup of Jell-O that his wife had put up for lunch, it occurred to him how unnaturally quiet these girls were. In three hours, there had not been so much as a peep. They huddled together in the center of the vehicle where the sun could not reach. Every now and then, they opened their bags pushed their heads in and nibbled at the food the nuns provided.

"I've got a couple of big sandwiches. I'm happy to share."

"Oh no," Mary said.

Jane continued, "Mother would be very upset if we ate more than allowed. We can wait."

***

Just before sunset, Andrew braked to a stop at 2805 Indian Hill Road by the arched entrance of the St. Bernard Cemetery. "This can't be right." He turned to the girls, "Show me the address."

Mary leaned forward so that he caught her sweet scent. He turned and caught her smile, perfect white teeth surrounded by red lips.

"Address is right." He shrugged.

"Of course," Jane said.

Mary nodded, "Let us out. Mother always waits for us here."

Then both together, "We are so hungry."

"I don't know." He said more to himself, but he climbed out of the cab, walked to the back, and helped them down. "Where is your mother?"

"We can show you." They charged ahead through the arched gate.

He followed them past the grave of John Pettigrew Delany, 1864-1869, Gone too soon. And then Mary Quincannon, Her red hair was her curse,

Born March 3, 1851. Died May 1, 1865. He stopped at the third with the headstone partially obscured by a large bush around which buzzed bees, Jane and Mary Doe, age 9. He shivered and said under his breath, "You're a damned fool, Andrew." There were so many graves, none of them new, not one less than twenty-five years old.

"She's in here," Mary waited by the iron door of a marble vault.

"Use the key." Jane smiled.

He wanted to ask what kind of mother met her children in a graveyard, but it was none of his business. He retrieved the key, slid aside the brass plate that protected the keyhole, and pushed the key in.

Mary leaned against him. "It's getting late."

Jane nodded, quiet, touching the paper label sewn to her lapel.

Andrew took a deep breath. "Maybe we should go into town. Look up a directory. I am sure your mother's address will be there somewhere.

Mary shook her head. "No, mother is always here."

"Where she always feeds us."

The lock resisted the key, as if the metal itself were reluctant to allow the living into the vault. He didn't want to force it, afraid it would break. So he jiggled the key and felt the mechanism give.

"Hurry. The sun is going down." The girls said together and crowded close.

Another jiggle of the key and the lock creaked.

The girl's soft breathing grew quicker. "What kind of mother," he said to himself, "fed her children in a crypt?" The girls did not answer.

He twisted the key harder and the locked turned.

"Open it," the girls said. It was likely stuck, so he turned the knob and pushed with his shoulder, and the door slipped open with ease. He shook his head. "Is this some kind of joke?" People had complained about the Postal Service delivering children. Maybe one of them had decided to pull a scam.

"Mother!" Mary and Jane called, and they ran through into the dark vault.

"Wait!" He called.

They didn't listen. Andrew fished into his mailbag, pulled out the cardboard tube flashlight the Post Office provided, and pushed the slide switch. Nothing.

He could not hear the girl's footsteps or their faint hurried breath. Patiently, he screwed the nickel plated end tight, and pushed the switch again. A beam of light illuminated dusty, black marble steps leading down, with leaves and other trash that had drifted into the corners of the steps. He walked, counting the steps while listening for the movements of Mary and Jane. At seventy, he reached a small square room, with four granite angels supporting the roof with their wings. In the center of marble walls to the right, left, and ahead, his flashlight illuminated the shapes of other doors.

Which way did they go?

He dragged the circle of light across the floor, looking for traces of their passage among the dust, spider webs, and the squat lozenge shapes of rat turds. Far as he could tell, no one had walked here in a quarter of a century. He turned and looked up the long flight of stairs. Faint light gleamed through the vault door above. He swept the walls, looking for an opening he'd missed in his hurry to reach the bottom. Nothing.

Turning again, Andrew shined his light into the vault, opened his mouth to call the girls but he could only manage a dry croak. After licking the inside of his mouth, he called again, "Mary? Jane?"

"Here," one of them answered, though he could not tell the direction.

He turned his head, searching for sound."

The other answered, "Yes, here."

The sounds came from the left. He found the door ajar.

"Just like children not to close it." He said, thankful for the sound of his human voice.

An engraved brass plate on the old door read, "May the door to death remain ever open for the passage of the living."

They must have built this vault before the Civil War, perhaps even before the Revolution. He had heard the stories of men buried alive and left to claw at the inside of their sealed caskets. Wealthy men, fearing death more than the loss of money, made sure that such a disastrous fate never happened to them. Taking the ring on the door in his hand, Andrew pulled. Though the hinges groaned, it remained shut.

Could the girls have fit through that narrow opening? He put his shoulder into it, and the ancient hinges creaked like an old man's arthritic bones. Two young girls could not have opened it. But they did wear those long dresses and woolen cloaks, and they were so light. Who knew how thin they were under their clothes?

Beyond the door, he found niches carved back into the bedrock that contained old coffins with names and dates of birth and death written on brass plates.

"Mary? Jane?"

They answered "Here," and he saw them at the edge of his light standing by a niche with its oak coffin in place. Had they been there a second ago? Probably just a trick of the darkness. Children had the knack of disappearing at will, especially when parents needed them.

"Where is your mother?" He allowed all the annoyance he felt throughout the long day creep into his voice. He was tired of the children, tired of their strangeness.

"She's here," Mary said, and waved at the coffin.

"Look, kid, this is a great joke, but the US Post Office does not deliver parcels to the dead. If your mother is not here to sign for you, I have to take you back.

"I'm here," came a whisper from behind. He spun around and his flashlight caught the pale face of a woman. She raised one hand to cover her eyes while the other pulled her hooded cloak tight against the vault's chill. He could just see a dark uneven line around her neck, like a necklace.

"Please." She said.

"Sorry." He flashed the light at their feet. Somehow, while he was not looking, the girls darted around him and stood close to their mother, their small bags in their hands.

"We are so hungry," Mary said.

"I know the sisters sent food with you." Their mother smiled.

"We ate it." Jane held up her bag.

"All of it." The mother raised her eyebrows.

Mary held up her bag. "I have this," She removed something thin and pale out of the bag, a child's finger with a bit of blood on the stub end. "I don't like this, mother. It's not fresh."

Andrew stared at Mary. This had to be a joke.

Their mother smiled. "It's so difficult to keep food fresh when we travel. You can throw it away, sweetheart. You brought dinner with you." She gestured past the girls.

Andrew backed away and then lifted the light. Mary Duchene turned her head sideways and smiled. "I am sorry, but I must feed my children. You understand."

Her hood slid back, exposing her neck and shoulders. That line, so like a necklace, opened. It looked as if someone at some time had cut her throat, severing the arteries, the larynx, and exposing the white bones of her spine.

Something coiled and slithered inside the neck, and long tentacle arms reached through the cut. Two of those arms, longer than the others, were like the long feedings arms of a squid, but with eyes where the suckers should be and gaping mouths on the flat pads at end ends.

Andrew turned to run. The woman and her daughters stood between him and the door. There had to be another way out.

He took his eyes off those little girls for only a second. That was enough. They swarmed around him, their hands grabbing at his pant legs, stopping him. Their plump child faces had become lean, feral. Their mouths gapped. Their white teeth gleamed. Tongues extended like feeding tentacles between their red lips, and where they touched him, his khaki pant leg ripped, and pain seared his flesh.

Andrew kicked at them, but his legs were stiff, wooden things. He shoved at the girls, but their solid, cloth covered flesh had grown soft and pliant. His hand sunk into their doughy flesh until he felt something inside, something ridged and hard that shifted and moved away.

Mary swatted him with her hand. It was like a punch from that heavy weight fighter he saw back in 1910, Jack O'Brien, and it knocked him back against the wall. Jane pummeled his chest with her balled fist, driving him to the floor. They swarmed over him, pliable, soft, with a hideous strength.

More tentacles with blinking eyes and gaping mouths pushed through their clothing, reached for him, wrapping his arms, tangling his legs, and gouging out divots of flesh. Andrew opened his mouth to scream and a feeding tentacle that tasted of ammonia and rotted fish slipped into his mouth. He vomited what remained of his lunch.

"Girls," Mother said.

They stopped eating, and the mouths on the ends of their feeding tentacles opened and answered, "Yes" in sweet, little girl voices.

"It is unladylike to bolt your food."

"Yes, mother."

"Take small bites. Chew your food before you swallow. Your dinner is going nowhere. We can make this meal last all night."

.

SPOOKLIGHT
Lance Davis

Lance is a married father of two from Northwest Arkansas and a long-time fan of the horror genre. His stories have been published by or appeared in: *Frightmares A Fistful of Flash Fiction, Gothic Blue Book III: The Graveyard Edition, Blood Reign Lit, The Twelve Nights of Christmas, Peripheral Distortions* by Death Throes Publishing, featured on the Death Throes Publishing webzine September issue, and *Bones II*. He can be found at: facebook.com/LanceDavisII.

It was a dark cloudy night as I looked down on Big Piney Creek in search of the Dover Lights. I was alone on the quiet lookout above the canyon. The only inhabitation nearby was the Long Pool Campground which was below the lookout but around a bend in the creek and not on the same hillside the lights are supposedly on. I had left my flashlight in the car in the hopes of better seeing them.

I was unsure of what to expect as I thought of the various stories surrounding this anomaly. The lights were said to appear and disappear among the trees as well as change colors. The stories surrounding them range from the ghosts of coal miners killed in a mine collapse in the 1800's to Spanish Conquistadors looking for gold to a Native American burial site, as well as others. As I pondered it, the first light appeared almost 1200 feet below me.

My heart raced as I stood near the edge of the hillside and watched the lone white light weave among the trees. It cruised near the trunks then flew upwards for a moment before slowly dropping back down again. Back and forth it repeated the cycle, never leaving my field of vision. The white turned red, then blue, green, then orange, and finally white again. Then it disappeared.

I scanned the darkness hoping the show was not over. Then saw it was again barely 1000 feet directly below me. It wavered back and forth alternating colors before going out again. It reappeared about 800 feet away then right back out.

I was getting nervous and considered jogging back to my car. I should have brought my flashlight. As it reappeared just below me I looked around and realized how utterly alone I was. I backed away from the overlook as it appeared just over the ledge.

The steady alternating of colors held me like a deer in the headlights. I wanted to bolt and run for my car but my feet felt as though they were cemented to the dirt path. There was nothing but me, the light, and deathly silence.

As it neared me, it elongated and stretched like a balloon, pulling itself thin before snapping into two. The two then stretched into four. The lights surrounded me. It was so blinding I dropped to my knees and covered my head. Through the shimmering waves I could swear I saw a dirty work boot. The light intensified and I closed my eyes tight.

Then came the noise. The beating sound of war drums filled my ears, the cry of women and horses, of men shouting, the pounding of waves on rocks, ships and blowing wind. A strange conglomeration of sound all mingled and muffled together. Laughter and screaming, rifle fire and cannon bursts.

Keeping my eyes closed tight, I put my hands to my ears but it did no good. It was getting inside me. I wanted to run but could only manage to quiver with my hands to my head. Then it was gone.

I was afraid to look. The dark was as overwhelming as the light. I listened for something or someone. After a moment, I finally picked up my head enough to peek out. The light was faint near the edge of the lookout. Slowly, I pulled myself to my feet. The light shifted as if someone turning their head to look at me.

I rubbed my eyes and when I pulled them away I found them covered in dirt. I rubbed the blackened smudge between my fingers. Clumps of dust fell off my clothes and drifted from my hair. I found myself amidst a circle of coal dust. A cool breeze picked up and blew it away. The light disappeared as if a miner turning off his lamp.

In the quiet, I realized it wasn't just one legend. It was all of them. Spanned by generations of time, these once men and women congregated together in this place. On hands and knees, I crept to the edge of the lookout for one final look. The canyon glowed.

MAKING FRIENDS
Nicole DeGennaro

Nicole DeGennaro currently works as a copy editor for a science publisher and lives in the Hudson Valley area of New York. Although she studied journalism at Purchase College, her heart has always belonged to fiction writing. Her short and flash fiction stories have been published in the anthologies *Scared Spitless, Gothic Blue Book III: The Graveyard Edition, The Grotesquerie* and *100 Worlds*. You can learn more about Nicole at her blog: nicoledegennaro.wordpress.com.

Beryl knelt in front of the headstone; the soft cemetery grass acted as a cushion between her shins and the cool soil separating her from the dead. She took a trowel out of her bag and laid it on the ground to her left. Then she pulled out a tattered book with a cover the color of a tanned hide. She placed it in front of her knees so that it rested between her and the headstone.

The full moon hung low and huge in the sky, just as it always did when Beryl came to the cemetery. She enjoyed being outside at night, when the other denizens of the town were asleep and would not notice or bother her. They all feared the dark and the creatures they believed it summoned, but she found what people did in daylight far more terrifying. Illegal activities needed the cover of darkness, but human cruelty could happen at any time.

She rubbed her upper arm, where a bruise waited to bloom from a well-aimed rock thrown at her earlier that day.

"Bizarre Beryl," the kids always yelled. "Who let you out alone?"

"Bizarre Beryl," others responded. "You should get back home."

Words, nothing but words—they would be harmless if not for the threat lurking behind the sing-song tone. She no longer remembered the number of times she had been driven back to her grandmother's house by a barrage of rocks and sticks, or a fleet of kids chasing her on their bikes.

When she had to venture out during the day, for school or errands, she tried to become invisible. But her taupe brown skin made her an anomaly in the small town, and nothing about her personality helped her fit in either.

No matter where she went in the daylight, a group of kids would follow her at a distance, a trailing white cloud comprising equal parts curiosity and malice. They all wanted to know what she was up to, but no one wanted to know Beryl.

Still, all the taunting and torture hadn't stopped her from making a friend.

"I'm here," she said to the headstone, leaning forward to run her hand over the engraved letters.

CANDICE LEGREW
SEPT. 13, 1940 – NOV. 13, 1953
Beloved for and cursed by her quirks

Beryl had heard the stories about Creepy Candice, as the townsfolk called her. Born on Friday the 13th and died on another Friday the 13th at age 13—cursed in every way, Beryl's grandmother said, making the sign of the cross over her chest whenever someone mentioned Candice.

Beryl didn't know whom the townspeople had ostracized between Candice's death and her own arrival, but the minute she had learned about Candice Legrew, she had felt a connection to the dead girl. She knew they would have been friends, and if they had had each other, it wouldn't have mattered what the other kids or the adults had to say about them. They could have snuck out of their rooms at night, done whatever they wanted together under the moon's protection.

After Beryl had skipped ahead one grade and then two in school, her teachers hadn't known what to do with her anymore. So, she had given herself a special task, and like most things in her life in the town, it involved Candice. Beryl wanted to get to know her predecessor, her missed friend. The small town library was mostly useless; even the archives for the local newspaper were ill-kept and incomplete. But by claiming she had a school research project, she had convinced her grandmother and a rotating roster of aunts, uncles and cousins who came to visit to take her on a few trips to the larger library in the nearby city.

There she had found many interesting snippets about Candice Legrew in the police blotter from the newspapers during her short life. She had frequently been caught trespassing in abandoned buildings at night, or lurking in neighbors' yards, or even wandering in the cemetery a few times.

But one instance in particular had snared Beryl's attention, had begun her routine almost a year ago of visiting Candice's tomb on the full moon. About three weeks before her death, Candice had been caught in the cemetery. The blotter had few details but claimed she had been defacing headstones and grave robbing. However, the newspaper had a "weird local news" section where an anonymous source inside the police department had elaborated on Candice's graveyard activities; they said she had been performing some kind of Satanic ritual. She had drawn complicated symbols on a headstone in her own blood and had dug a hole that almost reached the casket below. When the police had found her, she had been holding an old book and chanting in a weird language.

After that incident, the newspaper did not mention Candice again until her death, which had been as odd as her life.

Her parents had gone to a town meeting, knowing better than to bring Candice along by then. When they had returned home, all the doors and windows were still closed and locked; everything was as they had left it except their daughter, who had been dismembered in the basement. The list of suspects had been long, as so many people had wished harm upon her at some point, but no evidence had ever been found. For all anyone could tell, somehow Candice had dismembered herself.

Beryl reached down and picked up the old book; some of the pages had fallen out and been shoved back in, out of order, and an angry scorch mark ran up the back cover. She had rescued it from the rubble of the Legrew house, which had remained uninhabited after Candice's death and had burned down almost exactly a year after her burial. The fire department hadn't arrived in time, according to a newspaper article, although Beryl suspected the town had wanted the building destroyed. Once it had burned to the ground, nobody had ever cleaned up the debris.

Although the details of Candice's life provided by the newspapers fascinated Beryl, they hadn't been satisfying. She wanted to know more, wanted to know why Candice had died, or who had killed her. So she had started searching for remnants of her friend around the town—people often thought that once someone like Candice or Beryl moved on, their town went back to how it had been. But she knew that outcasts like her left a permanent impression just below the veneer of normalcy.

So Beryl had started with the obvious: Candice's grave and the Legrew house. She hadn't known which would yield more information first; it ended up being the remains of the house. Beryl still couldn't say what had made her start digging through the gnarled cinders, most of which had crumbled in her hands, stained her clothes sooty black and left her smelling of smoke for days. She had heard a voice, a whisper in the darkness calling out to her, and for a chilling moment she thought that all this time some part of Candice had been trapped in the debris, waiting for someone she could trust and befriend to dig her out.

Nothing had turned up on the first few nights of her efforts, but Beryl had kept sifting through the ash, wading through it, crawling on her hands and knees, until one night she reached the concrete foundation that still stood under the twisted skeleton. The entry to the basement had stared up at Beryl from the soot-covered floor like a dead eye, and waiting for her at the top of the stairs was the book, the one possession of the Legrews to survive the fire intact. Only the scorch mark scar hinted at what it had experienced.

She put the book in her lap and opened it to a page about one-third of the way through; it had first caught her attention because it stuck out at an angle and a few smeared fingerprints lurked in the margins. It had received a lot of attention from Candice, and thus it received all of Beryl's. A series of symbols, including a trowel and one of the familiar full moon, decorated the top of the page, followed by instructions written in a strange language— it seemed akin to but not exactly Latin. Beryl knew whatever Candice had been doing her last night in the cemetery had involved those words and runes.

Candice's frantic handwriting lined the margins of the page, some of it smudged by the fingerprints and rendered unreadable. Beryl didn't know how, but her friend had found a translation for the language—Candice's instructions had started the year-long adventure that would culminate by the end of the night.

To Raise The Dead
—Dig a hole so some part of the dead body is exposed to moonlight.
—Paint symbols onto headstone. IN BLOOD.
—Recite chant; pronunciations as follows…

"IN BLOOD" had been circled; Beryl wondered how many times Candice had tried the incantation with symbols in ink or paint before she discovered the missing ingredient.

But these were directions only for the final part of the ritual; during the preceding twelve months, Beryl had come to Candice's tomb and followed various other ceremonies as directed by translations in the book—all to ensure that when she raised her friend, Candice would be aware and in one piece, given the circumstances of her death. Beryl had written ancient runes on pieces of paper and buried them around the headstone, at the foot of the grave, and at various depths in the soil over the casket. She had chanted strange words while performing odd dances under the full moon and had sprinkled pungent herbs over the grass. It had all filled her with great joy; she had found a place she fit in and a task that suited her. If she had done everything correctly, in about an hour she would meet Candice for the first time.

Beryl set to digging with the trowel; the soil came up easily, as if it had been recently tilled, and filled the air with the rich scent of fertilizer. Perhaps some of her rituals had readied the ground, or maybe Candice herself had done something to facilitate her resurrection. Either way, she soon had a small hole dug, about a foot wide and three feet deep. Candice's black casket shone like a beetle carapace at the bottom. As Beryl prepared to use the trowel to try and crack through the lid, she noticed that part of the casing had already splintered outward, as if Candice had tried to break free. She grinned and leaned over the hole, sticking the sharp point of the trowel between some slivers of wood. Then she used it as a lever to break off pieces until she exposed the delicate cream lining inside. It tore away without much effort, and Beryl could see a bit of her friend's arm in the moonlight.

"Soon now, Candice," she whispered. "Just be patient a bit longer."

She placed the trowel to the side and reached into her bag, pulling out a cloth-wrapped parcel that she laid on the grass near the hole. Then she folded back the cloth to reveal a paring knife. She had sterilized the blade with rubbing alcohol before leaving her grandmother's house; the sharp smell of it burned her nose, cutting through the earthy aroma of the graveyard and the faint hint of rot that floated up from the casket. Without hesitating, she picked up the knife and cut a shallow gash in her left palm; the blood flowed quick and steady. For good measure, although the directions didn't call for it, she let a few drops fall onto the decaying flesh of her friend's arm. Then she set to work painting the symbols on the headstone. Some of her blood ran into the engraved words as she smeared on the complex shapes from the book.

When she finished, she wiped her fingers on the grass to get the blood off and tied the cloth around her palm to stanch the bleeding. Then, with the moon washing the cemetery in silver light, Beryl began to chant. Even though she had practiced, silently mouthing the words over the last week as she lay in her bed trying to fall asleep, her tongue still stumbled over the strange combinations of vowels and consonants. The night swallowed the words before they could get much further than her lips, but as she spoke the third line, a swift wind kicked up. It pulled her hair out of its ponytail and whipped it into her face, and the words spilled from her stronger and more solid, carried by the wind up toward the low full moon. Her bones started to vibrate as if from the beating of loud, ancient drums.

About halfway through the chant, a chorus of guttural and hissing voices joined her; the wind, still blowing strong, became hot and stank of organic decomposition, of once-solid things liquefying. The hair on the back of her neck rose, and she glanced around, but the cemetery remained empty except for her and the headstones. The chorus rang in her ears, drowned out her own voice. They chanted with knowledge, with certainty; it was their language, and it penetrated her skin, spread through her body like an incurable disease.

As the last part of the incantation left her lips and fled into the night, the wind and voices and drums disappeared with an abruptness that left a vacuum of silence. Beryl gasped and began to cry, for the first time in her life recognizing her loneliness. The chant and everything it had summoned had frightened her, but it had all been for her, because of her—an attention she had never been paid by anyone else. She looked down at the book and considered reading it again simply for the company.

Before she could, a black cloud drifted across the moon, shrouding the world in true darkness. Then it sank down, filling the graveyard like a polluted fog until Beryl could not see Candice's headstone or even the book that sat in her own lap. But she kept her eyes open, hoping to catch a glimpse of when her friend rose from the dead.

The cold fog swirled around her; she shivered as it pulled at her clothes and hair and the pages of the book. It wiped away the stench from the hot wind, replacing it with an odd metallic odor so strong she tasted it in the back of her throat. The world materialized again as the cloud disappeared into her friend's open grave. After a moment, the ground underneath her shook. She scrambled away, clutching the book against her chest. The soil and grass over the casket exploded outward as a tornado burst forth, towering into the night sky and sucking up any loose items, including Beryl's bag, trowel and paring knife. The tip of the tornado remained in the tomb, and coffin splinters and satin scraps spun in the darkness. Then the tornado blew apart with a sound like a thunderclap, embedding shards of wood in the ground all around the cemetery. Beryl suffered only a few small cuts and scrapes from bits of debris. She didn't see the trowel or knife anywhere, but her bag had been skewered and pinned to the ground near her feet by a gleaming fragment of Candice's casket.

The moon sat high in the sky, marking a greater passage of time than Beryl had expected. She wondered if Candice's resurrection had altered the spin of the Earth; she would almost believe that before accepting that so many hours had passed since the end of the chant.

She stood up and brushed herself off. For all the tumult, Beryl saw no sign of her friend. With a frown, she approached the destroyed gravesite, inching around bits of wood, satin and other detritus she couldn't identify.

Before she reached the edge of the large hole, a pale hand reached up from the grave and took hold of the bottom of the headstone, which had been cracked in half by the tornado. Then another hand appeared, and Candice used her damaged headstone to pull herself out of her tomb.

Beryl froze, staring wide-eyed, hardly believing that the chant had worked, that her friend now stood before her. Her tattered red gingham dress hung off her partly decomposed body; a dingy red bow held back the few remaining clumps of her blonde hair. Sloppy black stitches stood out against her green-gray skin at the knees, ankles, elbows, wrists and neck. The reassembly appeared to be the result of Beryl's rituals—Candice's right foot faced backward, a mistake a mortician would not have made, and her head had a permanent tilt to the far left that started where it had been reattached to her neck. Despite the imperfections, Beryl considered her work a success.

"Candice!" she said, moving forward until she stood across from her undead friend, only the pit of Candice's former grave separating them. With unsteady movements, Candice turned, bracing herself on her broken headstone. One eye socket sat empty, reminding Beryl of the gaping basement entrance where she had found the old book. The remaining eye had a sickly yellow sclera and a foggy brown iris. A large part of her face on the right side had decayed away, revealing her jaw, some teeth and the curve of her empty eye socket. "I'm your friend Beryl. I'm the one who brought you back."

Candice didn't move or speak, but Beryl could see the remnants of her tongue working through the hole in her face, trying to form words. She took a step toward Beryl, and her reassembled left knee bent at an incorrect angle. But she stayed on her feet, and after a moment she took her hand from the headstone. Beryl smiled as her friend stood on her own with no support; she had always known Candice would be strong, capable.

"Friend..." Candice said, her voice like old paper catching fire. Despite Candice's slurred speech, Beryl was certain she had said "friend."

"Right! I think we're going to have a lot of fun." She held up the book; when Candice glanced at it, the cover squirmed under Beryl's fingers. Then her one eye looked back at Beryl, and what was left of her lips pulled into a smile that was not friendly. But Beryl couldn't tell because she had never had a friend.

"Yes," Candice said, the word crackling like a spark. "Fun."

SCHOOL NIGHTS
James Dorr

Indiana writer James Dorr's *The Tears Of Isis* was a 2013 Bram Stoker Award® nominee for Superior Achievement in a Fiction Collection. Other books include *Strange Mistresses: Tales Of Wonder And Romance, Darker Loves: Tales Of Mystery And Regret,* and his all-poetry *Vamps (A Retrospective).* For more, readers are invited to visit Dorr's blog at jamesdorrwriter.wordpress.com.

Some people swore that the house was haunted. She didn't know why. Grownups were strange sometimes in the things they said. Like how the Earth was supposed to be round—but how come people on the other side didn't fall off then? Or how there were oceans so big you couldn't see across them.

When she was older, she learned the Earth *was* round. Oceans were big too. But still they claimed the house was haunted, and she didn't know how.

She had studied once to be a witch, or at least she thought she had. She'd read a book she had found in the library. She wasn't a witch, though. She knew that afterward.

She went to the house to determine, finally, whether the house was haunted or not. It was spooky and old, that was certainly true, and it had been deserted for many years, but search as she would she could find no ghosts. There were bodies of old people, homeless men mostly, beneath the window of one of the ground-floor rooms. Some were dried out, with no blood left in them, but a few were fresher.

There were rats and spiders too, and these were special ones. These ones talked to her.

"What is your name?" one said.

"Marcie," she answered. The spider who'd asked her looked ancient and crusty.

"Do you like blood?" an odd, winged rat asked.

Marcie shrugged. She'd never tried blood. But some of the newer, plumper corpses looked juicy like ripe fruit. When she thought that, her teeth started to itch, the sharp, pointed ones near the front of her mouth on either side of the flat, chiseled front ones.

Nothing was ever the same again after that.

DOWN BY THE RIVER
Christina Glenn

Christina Glenn is a biology student by day and a closet writer by night. She grew up in Wilmington, North Carolina, fed heavily on the city's ghost stories, which gave her a lifelong love of all things supernatural. Horror is her favorite genre, especially the works of H.P. Lovecraft and Arthur Machen.

No matter how I hid under my blankets, or buried myself in a closet, I could not hide from the monster that would come for me. Her breath would be sour with whiskey and her hands would swing freely, leaving me bruised and broken night after night.

One night, I ran from her–ran until I had nothing left in my body. When she found me, her wrath fell down upon me like a thousand angry gods, and then she left me. I could not walk, so I clutched the bare earth with my broken hands and dragged myself until the darkness took me. When I awoke, the pain in my body was such that it fought every motion I tried to make, but I did not let it stop me. Again and again I would wake and pull myself as far as I could, but, in the end, I always succumbed to the darkness.

I came, finally, to a cemetery by a river, long forgotten by any who may have cared for those buried beneath. Here I heard a weeping, a sound which echoed centuries of grief and torment. The sound filled my soul with sorrow and a cry rose in my throat. From behind a crumbling headstone a figure in white rose, magnificent and shining. She moved towards me and lifted me in her arms, water dripping from her body and soaking through my skin.

"My child?" her lips met my forehead, cold and moist. "You shall be my child, now."

I felt water pooling under my skin, crushing my already broken bones. A scream of pain tried to escape my lips, but water cascaded out instead. I could not fight her, I was too tired of fighting.

"Quiet now, dearest," she stroked my hair, "There is no more need of weeping or pain for us."

She carried me into the water, and we slowly submerged. The world above me distorted, yet my vision cleared. I could see her now as she was, her beautiful face twisting and bloating, a corpse that had been too long in the water. Her weight pressed me down, deeper and deeper into the darkness. Always into the darkness. Yet, I no longer felt pain or fear. I was her daughter now, and the darkness was our home.

HUNTING THE DEVIL
Agustin Guerrero

Agustin Guerrero was raised on werewolf stories and urban legends in Southern Florida. He has recently self-published his first novel, The Amalgam. You can find more of his work at agustinguerrero3.wordpress.com, where there are links to the other social medias.

Charlie holds up two silent fingers, then one. When he points at me the world blurs at the periphery and a familiar calm washes over me.

"Good evening, folks. This is Mike Adams and I want to thank you for joining me tonight out in New Jersey's Pine Barrens. On this edition of *Finding Cryptos*, we'll be on the hunt for the creature known as the Jersey Devil."

Charlie gives me a thumbs up and I turn and walk deeper into the pines. I hear Sophia moving close behind me, holding the boom mic just out of the shot. Our producer and a group of volunteer 'Crypto Hunters' are slamming through the underbrush. I continue.

"Now, we're about a mile outside of the area known as Leeds Point, the so-called birthplace of the Jersey Devil. Legend has it that the Leeds family lived out here in the early 1700s." I pause and step over a particularly large branch. The route we're taking could barely be called a path. It's more like a group of stubborn patches that refuse to succumb to the forest.

"Mrs. Leeds was apparently a very… ah… fertile woman. She had already given birth to twelve children and had a thirteenth on the way. Her previous children had given her no trouble when they came into the world. It was clear this one would be a different case. Mrs. Leeds was screaming in pain all through the evening, though she had birthed her previous children in near silence. The sound was almost inhuman. Finally, around midnight, she brought a monstrosity into the world. A horned head adorned a spindly body, with two leathery wings protruding from its spine. The creature stared up at her from a puddle of amniotic fluid as the family looked on from around her bed. Her scream was mirrored by the abomination before it flew up their chimney, the sound ringing through the night. Locals say when the moon is full, the screams still echo through Leeds Point. Lucky for us, there's a full moon rising."

I make a cutting motion across my neck and Charlie lowers the camera. Sophia sighs in relief as she lowers the boom mic. I stop and wait for the rest of the volunteers to catch up.

"Charlie, do you think you could get a shot of the moon coming up over the trees?"

"Yeah, sure thing," the burly man replies as he moves silently for a better angle. I haven't quite figured out how such a bear of a man can make so little noise. Cameramen like him are few and far between. Sophia moves closer to me, collapsing the unwieldy microphone.

"So, the Jersey Devil," she says looking at me. "Do you think we're actually going to find anything this time?"

"As long as our viewers think so, we'll be fine."

I look toward the group of volunteers as they approach. They're mostly men in their late thirties, with a few women in the same age group. These are our typical hunters.

"We've gotta make this one convincing," I say out of the corner of my mouth, "I hope you're ready."

I open my arms and smile as Rodney joins us in the clearing. My producer is flushed from the short hike. He'll be manning our base camp while we take the hunters out. Sophia hands him a water bottle from her bag and he gulps it down greedily. The rest of the volunteers are circling around us.

"Glad you could make it out B-Rod," I say and slap him on the back. He waves me off and continues guzzling water. I turn to address the rest of the crowd.

"Fellow crypto hunters, I recognize some of you from our previous hunts. This makes me believe you're half-crazy to follow us around the country. Good, you've gotta be a little crazy for this gig."

I pause for the forced laughs from the group. A few remain silent.

"Tonight we're going to be splitting into teams. My cameraman Charlie and I will be taking two volunteers with us. We're going to look for the old Leeds house. Sophia and my good friend B-Rod will be remaining here at our now official base camp. The rest of you break into two teams of three." The group looks amongst themselves, automatically grouping with the hunters they know best. One pair looks a little out of place. I wave them over as the other groups form around them.

"Alright looks like we're divided. Each group take a walkie talkie and a GPS tracker. If you see anything out of the ordinary, call it in on channel 3. Grab your gear, leave what you don't need, and let's get huntin'." I raise a hand and let out the howl we'd claimed as our trademark. The other hunters mirror my howl. I turn and see Charlie grinning despite the howl pouring from his throat.

We click on our flashlights and move north toward the supposed location of the Leeds' home. I can't imagine there will be anything left after three centuries, but the viewers expect a thorough investigation. Charlie has attached the boom mic to his camera and is filming the woods around us. The last shreds of sunlight die out as we pick our way through the pines.

"So," I say to the couple, "are you two new to the hunt?"

"Not exactly. We were fans of the last season and we live in the area so we figured, you know, why not?" The woman laughs while her partner nods.

"Alright, well why don't you introduce yourselves to the camera?" I say as Charlie turns the camera on them. They slow down and look at each other.

"My name is Lauren Decatur and this is my brother, Steve." The woman tells the camera. The two stare into the lens for a few moments before Steve breaks into an awkward smile. I sigh inwardly and prompt them.

"So tell us why you're here tonight."

"We're here to find the Jersey Devil," Steve answers "and when we find it, I'm going to put a bullet in its horned head."

He moves his jacket and I can see a sidearm holstered there. My heart starts beating faster.

"Uh...Steve I think you might have taken the title a little too literally. The show's called *Crypto Hunters* because we're looking for them, not poaching them."

"This is personal," he says and lowers the flap of his jacket. I look over at Charlie but the big man is as impassive as ever. I take a breath.

"Okay Steve, just keep that thing holstered, alright buddy? I don't want anybody getting hurt tonight." He doesn't respond and after a few seconds Charlie lowers the camera. He looks over at me and I shake my head slowly. *Where does Rodney find these people?*

After a few more minutes of hiking, we arrive in a clearing. Dancing beams of light reflect off of what looks to be the burned foundation of a long forgotten home.

"Holy shit," I say and motion toward Charlie, "this has to be the place. Who else would be living all the way out here?" Charlie gives me a silent countdown and I slip into my television persona.

"We've just come upon the remains of the Leeds' home, deep in the Pine Barrens. The house appears to have burned down long ago. Perhaps the hellfire of the Jersey Devil's birthing consumed the home? Let's move in for a closer look."

As Charlie and the Decaturs move toward the foundation, I quietly pull the walkie talkie from my pack. I change the channel from three to four and whisper softly into the mic.

"Now."

I slip the walkie back into the pack and hurry to catch up with the group. I manage to get back into the shot before a scream echoes through the trees.

"What was that?" I whirl around to face the camera, eyes wide in staged fear. Charlie sweeps the camera lens over the trees behind us before focusing on the Decaturs. Lauren has a hand over her mouth, her pupils shifting back and forth with almost comical speed. Steve moves his hand toward the holster, jaw set. I pull out my walkie talkie and switch to channel three.

"A bloodcurdling scream has just pierced the air somewhere to the south. I'm attempting to raise our base camp," I say loud enough for the mic to pick me up.

"Base, this is Adams. Did you hear that?"

"Mike," Sophia's voice squawked, "that scream was close to us. I'm calling in the other groups." Her voice is tinged with just the right amount of trepidation. The Decaturs look to me and I wave them forward. I switch the walkie back to channel four and hit the button twice. Another scream comes from our camp a few moments later.

"We may have found it," I shout to the camera, "the Jersey Devil itself m—."

A second scream answers from much closer. I spin toward the sound and lose my footing, crashing into Charlie. The big man hardly moves as I bounce off him toward the ground. I can't even feel the impact. The adrenaline pushes me to my feet and I lock eyes with Charlie. Something flies overhead, too fast to be caught by our flashlight beams.

"Hey wait up," I shout to the Decaturs. Charlie and I run to catch up with the jogging siblings. The camera light bounces between trees, filming forgotten as we approach the camp. A shriek crashes out of Lauren's throat when she sees the remains. I arrive a few steps behind her and feel genuine terror grip my stomach contents, wrenching them from my mouth with a powerful heave. The half-digested sandwich I'd had for dinner splashes over my boots. I look up through watering eyes at what's left of camp.

Sophia's head rests a foot away from her body, blood pooling underneath. Her face looks passive; she didn't have time to react to the vicious attack. Rodney is another story.

Resting against a nearby pine are the remnants of our producer. Twin holes are drilled into his chest, dark blood staining rivers down his white shirt. His mouth is frozen in twisted agony as one of his eyeballs dangles from its socket. His arms are a mess of bloodied wounds. I stare at my dead friends while the sandwich congeals on my shoe. Another scream brings me back to reality.

One of the volunteers runs through the campsite, being chased by something massive. All we can do is watch as the volunteer is grabbed and hoisted by his neck, legs kicking uselessly in the air. The creature smashes his face into a nearby tree, wood splintering from the impact. His lifeless body falls to the ground and the monster turns to face us.

The Jersey Devil is described as a skinny creature with a goat's head and bat wings. Somebody got it wrong. The head does resemble a ram, but in addition to the curled rams' horns, twin jagged spikes protrude from its head. It stands taller than Charlie, white fur covering its considerable bulk. Two giant wings unfold from its back as the creature takes a step forward and lets out a scream.

Steve reacts first. He unholsters his gun with practiced speed and draws a bead on the creature's chest. The rest of us react a second later and we run back the way we'd come. We hear the battle behind us, the staccato echo of small arms fire punctuating the screams.

Just as suddenly as they'd begun, the screams and gunshots stop. Whether there is a victor or Steve has simply run out of bullets we can't tell. We just keep running.

Lauren's conscience catches up with her and she slows her pace, forcing Charlie and me to slow behind her. She looks at me and I see unspoken pleading in her eyes. I know she needs to go back to the camp, to see if her brother somehow survived.

Charlie pushes past her and continues to run back toward the Leeds' home. I'm right behind him. Lauren is yelling after us, calling us all the names she can think of. We don't stop. A scream sounds behind us, cutting through the night. It could be Lauren.

We run into the clearing and slow a little, trying to catch our breath.

"Oh God, what are we going to do?" I'm jogging toward the burned out foundation. Charlie doesn't answer. I feel him close behind as I reach the site of the creature's birth. There's not much in the way of cover, the years turning the wooden framework to dust. There seems to be an opening that leads underground. I make for it.

I'm only a few feet away when a scream sounds from overhead. I skid to a stop as the creature slams down in front of me. The force of the landing permeates through the ground before it begins to rise. I start to back up and run into Charlie. His bulk offers too little resistance and his mountainous body crumbles and falls. A gaping hole in his chest is barely visible as the camera crashes to the ground. The camera light shatters and Charlie disappears into darkness. My own flashlight illuminates the beast as it bites into Charlie's heart, blood squirting from his aorta in three equal streams.

Instinctively, I take a step back. Instinct forgets that Charlie's body is directly behind me and I trip over his remains. I go down hard and the air explodes from my lungs. My head hits the ground and my vision momentarily goes white. Blinded, I claw at the ground behind me. I'm struggling to draw in a breath but my diaphragm is openly rebelling. As my vision begins to clear I see the creature stalking toward me. It's opening its mouth to let loose another one of its ear-shattering shrieks. A flood of erratic thoughts strike me as I continue crawling backwards. Had any of the volunteers made it? Would the footage from the night ever be found? Who would play me if they found the footage and made the movie?

The creature releases the scream it had been building, but it wasn't the one we'd been hearing through the night. This one was at a lower pitch. It didn't sound as feral somehow. I feel the first dangerous threads of hope course through my veins. I continue to crawl, but the beast has stopped pursuing.

I feel the rush of air before I hear the flapping of another immense set of wings. I turn and look up to see another monster half illuminated in my forgotten flashlight. It's larger than the Jersey Devil, black fur covering its muscled body. The monster's red eyes meet mine and I see the head is lacking horns. The strings of hope are ripped from my body, leaving me a dangling marionette of despair. I try to roll away but one hoof pins me to the ground. I let out my first scream of the night.

A brood of miniature goat creatures are climbing from the new arrivals' back. They swarm over me, covering my body in an instant. I feel the individual stabbing pains of their bites from a dozen sites on my body. Their mother continues to pin me down and my flailing slows. I can see the dark clouds of death in my periphery. Before the darkness consumes me, I hear a chorus of screams in the distance.

SEASIDE BOUND
Emma Hinge

Emma Hinge is a literary enthusiast, who occasionally puts pen to paper. Her short stories can be found in anthologies by Burial Day Books and The Alchemy Press. She lives in Christchurch, New Zealand with her boring engineer husband and a bed-hog cat. You can find her on twitter @missoilcan.

"I'm still not sure about this, doctor."

"Then it is just as well you are not paid for your opinions, Margaret. Tighten those arm-cuffs, if you will."

"But William! It's just-"

"No; it is *not just* anything, nurse. My diagnosis is final, and so is this treatment plan. And may I remind you that your current behaviour gives me grounds enough to ask the medical board for your dismissal. Now the mouthpiece, if you please." The doctor outstretches a confident hand, without once looking up from the patient beneath him. The stocky woman whom he had addressed rubs her palms against the stiff fabric of her starched uniform, before reluctantly picking up the rubber mouthpiece from the medical trolley to her left. She places the item tentatively upon the cracked, dry fingers of the man that towers over her. Strapped to the frame beneath, a girl with green eyes stares straight into his with hot, unblinking blame. The nurse chews at a scraggly fingernail. Then she shifts from one foot to the other. She knows how uncommon it is for a senior physician to oversee such a routine treatment, and although she has attempted to ignore it, she can't help but feel uneasy about the morally unnerving manner in which those green eyes stare.

While Margaret has worked at the *Seaside Women's Mental Rehabilitation Centre* for a little over seven years, this moment is the first in which she has felt a direct sense of accountability for the care of a patient. She scrunches her toes up uncomfortably tight in her shoes as she attempts to rationalise her feeling of unease. She wonders if perhaps her nervousness has developed as a result of the unusual way in which this girl was admitted.

After all, the girl seemed to have just turned up, delivered without warning by two policemen in the middle of a nightshift; where she was subsequently cast straight into solitary room 410 on the fourth floor. Or, Margaret thought, perhaps it was because of the girl's age. At thirteen, Catherine was by far the youngest patient that Margaret had treated in her work at the *Seaside Women's Mental Rehabilitation Centre*. Irrespective of either of these unusual instances, Margaret concluded that there was definitely something illogically ominous in the air that made her feel that she would regret this moment. And indeed, such a warning was completely exotic to a woman who, for the past seven years, had been explicitly trained out of trusting in her own intuition.

Margaret begins to clench her teeth as she watches Doctor William Casey attach the electrodes on either side of those green eyes. She watches as William fidgets with the settings on the machine, muttering to himself with the patient file held close against his chest. And she watches as his muttering stops and the dial is turned clockwise, his attention barely registering the numbers spaced cyclically from one to ten. But as William Casey's index finger pushes down on the critical red button with a discriminatory click, Margaret looks away. The eleven-seconds that Margaret stares at the overhead clock-face seem to her to be the longest of her life. As the thin hand clicks agonisingly forward, Margaret is overwhelmed by indescribable dread. For the first time in her relatively uneventful middle-aged life, Margaret Walker feels that she is exactly eleven seconds closer to death.

***

The faded yellow glow of the overhead streetlight illuminates the forms of two unobtrusive figures. The figures stand close, collecting currents of confidence as they consider the derelict shell of the fenced-off four-storied building before them.

"If my dad finds out that I pinched his bolt-cutters, I am *so* dead," one figure protests.

"Yeah, yeah; you've only said that about a million times. Quit being such a pansy about it. He's not going to find out," replies the other, taller figure. Their collective gaze fixates upon the padlocked gate in front of them.

"I'm just saying, James. I'd be literally dead. Then where would you be?" The shorter figure looks to his friend, down to the padlock, and then beyond the barbed-topped fence to the shadowed monstrosity of the brick building. Choked with overgrown ivy, the walls stir restlessly in the ravaged saltiness of the wind. Max's arms prickle and he shivers as he lifts the pincers of the bolt-cutters to the curved bar of the padlock.

"Well you never know though, Max." James contemplates, chewing audibly on a wad of flavoured gum. "We are breaking into an old crazy house, after all. If your old man *did* kill you, then you'd probably come back as a ghost or something anyway." James jabs his companion in the sides to articulate his point just as Max cuts through the slender arm of the padlock on the netted wire gate. Max squirms out of his friend's grip, his spine crawling.

"Don't; dickhead! I'm not gunna do this if you're gunna try to scare the shit out of me every five minutes." A retaliatory punch hits home in the centre of James's arm. Max takes note as James grimaces, his face flinching fleetingly. As James hastily attempts to brush off his embarrassment with a half-hearted laugh, he starts to feel the dull ache of a new bruise convulsing beneath his skin.

"So are we doing this, or not?" Max twists the clasp of the broken padlock free from the gate and kicks at the frame. The jangling sound of metal hangs in the air as nostalgic hinges swing inwards with a rusty groan. Both boys look up to the tired building before them. Both boys momentarily hesitate before stepping forward, each hoping the other had failed to suspect them of their awkward second of unease.

The boys scan the walls of slowly disintegrating brick. The ivy rustles, breathing, as waves of wind whistle in from the cooling sea. Together the boys walk around the building's borders, searching for a way inside. Before long they notice that the unhinged back door is jammed precariously into its frame. The sun-faded red lettering on the **NO ADMITTANCE** sign is barely visible beneath the sterile white light of their cell phones. Together they extract the door from its niche and rest it against the ivy covered brick. Devoid of its door, the cavity of the doorframe looks barren. No clear division exists between outside and in, and the boys step over the lip of the threshold noticing nothing of the change in the atmosphere.

Inside, the air is heavy with the smell of damp decaying wood. A few sheets of browned paper clatter down the hallway as salty air rustles in from the cavity of the removed door. Max composes himself, breathing in deeply before stepping further inside. He sweeps his illuminated cell phone screen around in the unexplored darkness, casing out the length of the hallway. A little more confident in his surroundings, he exhales methodically and grasps at a clipboard hung next to a locked door and inscribed with the words: *Staff Only*.

"Weird," Max states. "I don't think I actually expected this place to look so…*abandoned*." Max rustles through the papers on the clipboard with one hand. James snorts, grabbing a punch-card and testing it in the slot of the broken mechanical clock.

"Right. So the whole *abandoned mental hospital* thing didn't give you any clues, huh?" James sniggers, placing the punch-card back in its envelope before he proceeds to pick out a new one.

"Whatever, dude," Max replies, distracted by the papers on the clipboard. A pause hangs in the air as both boys consider their objects.

"Oi, James. Do you know why they stopped using this place, anyway?"

James looks down at his punch-card, considering. He flips it over in his hands, and then replaces it before answering.

"My dad said something about malpractice or whatever once. Dunno if that'd cause them to shut the whole place down though." James selects another card. "Eww, gross! I think there's blood on this one…"

"Urgh, let me see!"

The boys both look at the punch-card, and its three smeared fingerprints of brownish red. They study it; searching the illegibly faded black ink for any clues that could account for the cards misfortune. They flip it over. Printed in small handwritten capitals is a name.

MARGARET WALKER

The boys look to one another, the name caught in cowardly whispers on their lips. As James furiously stuffs the card back into its envelope, they both exhale quickly with a sigh of relief.

***

There were no words in Margaret Walker's vocabulary that she felt could accurately describe the intense curiosity that obsessed her. In fact, all but one of her fingernails had been chewed down to unpleasantly painful stubs as she struggled to understand her very uncharacteristic urge. Never before had she felt even marginally compelled to enter a doctor's office without express permission. Not because doing so could lead to her instant dismissal, but simply because such an impolite act just wasn't in her bookish nature. Besides, Margaret thought, she didn't care particularly vehemently - if at all - for many of the doctors that worked at the *Seaside Women's Mental Rehabilitation Centre;* and so subsequently she had held very little interest in what they happened to house in their offices. Or at least that was the case until her rather unusual encounter with Dr. William Casey and the green-eyed patient. Since then, Margaret had found herself obsessed with a fabricated fiction of secret patient files, police corruption and back-room deals. At night she dreamt of nothing but searching William's desk for hidden drawers, whilst during the day she found herself pulled ever closer to his office door and its elusive contents; often re-routing her paths from task to task in order to pass by it.

So it was with anxiety that Margaret observed her own curiosity as it grew relentlessly inside her. It was a bright and insignificant spring morning the day that curiosity peaked. As Margaret walked briskly down the eastern first-floor corridor, she felt a need to stop outside Dr. William Casey's office that was entirely insatiable. It was only as she slowed to a halt that she detected the sensation of being pushed by something that lay completely beyond her own rational explanation. Her stomach filled with knots of trepidation as her hand was wrenched from her own cognitive control. She closed her eyes and felt the coolness of the polished brass doorknob under the embrace of her fingers. Its shape felt smooth and comforting, and as she turned the gleaming round orb clockwise she heard a sharp click as the mechanistic lock gave way beneath her touch.

As Margaret stepped into the forbidden, she moved without seeing. Her fingers searched for fake bottoms to desk drawers as her eyes scanned for possible hiding places. She overturned potted plants and ripped paintings off the walls as she searched for something that to her rational self was unknowable. It was not long before she found her forefinger and thumb holding the cold, hard metal of a neatly shaped lockbox key. The lockbox she had already found, hidden in the bottom of Dr. Casey's patient filing cabinet. The moment that Margaret turned the key in its corresponding lock she knew that her fate had somehow been sealed. She woke from a trance to find herself staring down at the patient file of the green-eyed Catherine Burgess.

"I do not think this looks good for you, Margaret." Dr. William Casey stood with his broad shoulders blocking the only exit to the office. "I must say I am surprised. I never picked you for the snooping type. How very unfortunate," Dr. Casey took off his glasses and wiped them with a clean corner of the sleeve of his white overcoat.

"I really did hope that it would not come to this." Slowly he looped the tender arms of his glasses back over his ears. His convulsed face grew steely. He lowered his voice to a whisper.

"But I really don't have any choice."

***

Max and James move cautiously down dusty corridors, delving into unlocked rooms, prying open cabinets and desk drawers. All except one of their salvaged souvenirs they swung in carelessly flung open backpacks. Expertly excavated from a wayward box of confiscated goods, a hipflask was passed from one to the other. With each reciprocal swig, their nonchalance grew.

"These offices are getting boring," said James. "Where did they keep the crazies, anyway? That's what I really wanted to see this place for." He takes a swig from the hipflask.

"The floor plan on that staff clipboard said the patient rooms are all upstairs," Max replies.

"Hmm. Probably to keep them all in I guess. Wanna go up and have a look?" James asks enthusiastically.

"May as well." Shrugs Max.

***

Two men walk in through the back door of the *Seaside Women's Mental Rehabilitation Centre*. They stride down the hallway side-by-side, casually stepping over rotted floorboards and abandoned medical equipment.

"They should've known kids would get into this place eventually. A damned abandoned wacky hospital! I won't tell you a lie, Inspector Davis, if I was fifteen again this would be the first place I'd want to check out."

The Inspector grunts, pulling a small notepad out of his top breast pocket.

"So how long had the boys been missing?" The second man enquires, rustling in a backpack for a notepad of his own. The inspector raises his eyebrows questioningly.

"I thought you would have done your research on this one, Mike." He states, with an undertone of disappointment. "It was a little on two days. Wasn't until a local lass saw that the gate was busted open that we thought they might be holding up here."

"Right." Replies Mike, frantically scrawling the details down. "So what exactly...*happened?*"

"Well, to be honest, we still don't have much of an idea," sighs the Inspector. "That's where I thought you could come in. We need you to strike up a press release, try to bring in some information."

"Of course. That's what I do best," Mike replies, digging around in his coat pocket for a voice recorder.

"Just so you know we do suspect that there was someone else involved." The inspector flicks off his tinted glasses from their resting place on his forehead. The men make their way up the stairwell, climbing up the four flights of stairs. As they near the top, the inspector wheezes, out of breath from their climb. Mike looks to him with uncertainty.

"The bodies were taken out this morning but I'm warning you now – you're not going to like what you see." The inspector leads him through the hallway to the door of room 410.

"Strange history, this place has," grunts the Inspector. He places his hand on the handle, and turns. "Some nurse was murdered here once. Now people say it's haunted. Maybe they're not wrong."

Mike glances into the room and turns a pale shade of yellow. As nausea sweeps over him, the edges of his vision turn to black. Before he falls, the Inspector grabs him by the scruff of the neck, easing him down to the floor.

In the ceaseless nightmares that follow, Mike is haunted by fervent voices, muffled screams, bitten nails, and unnaturally green eyes.

BUS STOP
Kelly Hoolihan

Kelly Hoolihan is a marine biologist by day and a writer by nights and weekends. She has been published previously in *HWA Poetry Showcase volume 1* and she can be found on Twitter at @khooliha.

The bus was late. Luke and Charlie sat in the hunched over plexiglass stop. Dirt smeared the glass, obscuring the already weak sunlight. Charlie stared blankly into the middle distance while Luke tapped his foot impatiently. The soda bottle in Luke's hand was no longer sweating, and now the soda inside was just warming up to the ambient temperature around him. The day was colder than he thought it was going to be, though that could probably be blamed on the cloud cover and the unintentionally shady bus stop. Still, why hadn't he grabbed a jacket?

Next to him Charlie didn't seem to be feeling the cold. His friend had, some minutes before, pulled a cigarette out of his crumpled pack but instead of lighting it he let it just hang from his lips. Luke wondered how he could always be still. Luke would be fidgeting with his lighter as soon as he needed it for the cigarette, if not before. Charlie was always still and quiet and normally it was comfortable. Today, though, it was grating against Luke's nerves. He ground his teeth together and glanced back at the road. Still nothing.

"When the fuck is the bus coming?" Luke said, more to start a conversation than to express any sincere burning anger. Charlie grunted noncommittally, continuing to stare off into space. Luke swirled the remaining swallows of soda at the bottom of his bottle. Behind him, in the graveyard he always studiously avoided looking at whenever he used this bus stop, he heard the sound of a procession, soft footsteps on gravel, and muffled weeping. He continued to ignore the plot of land. Instead he turned slightly and looked down the road, wondering where the bus was. Flies buzzed around his head, too lazy to be much of an irritant.

"Seriously–how long have we been waiting here?" He looked at his watch, then back at the road, which was empty. Charlie shrugged and turned away slightly, apparently trying to avoid the conversation topic.

Luke turned back to the road, away from his friend, irritation rising. The bus was nowhere to be seen and Charlie was apparently in some mood. He didn't feel like letting it go. "Fuckin' bus," he muttered. "It's going to make us wait here all damn day."

"No, it won't." Charlie muttered in return. Luke began to slosh his mostly-empty bottle back and forth rhythmically. At the sound Charlie started slightly, then stared at the object. Luke watched Charlie's brows draw together and his face tighten. He realized that Charlie wasn't just in a mood—he was *angry*. But as quickly as Luke had noticed the emotion drained from Charlie's face. Now he just looked tired, like he'd been out all night and was paying the price today.

"What is it man?" Luke asked and his own irritation and impatience fell away. "What did I do?"

"Nothin'," Charlie said, but he didn't ease up, didn't turn away again.

"Come on," Luke persisted. "You have to tell me what's wrong." He tapped his bottle against his leg and Charlie focused again, seeming almost hypnotized by the movement.

"We're nothin' but a few swallows of warm soda and a couple holes in the ground." Charlie's voice was angry again and his hands were clenched and Luke couldn't help but draw back at the sudden, harsher display of emotion.

"Jesus man, what the fuck does that even mean? What crawled up your ass?"

Charlie looked at him, eyes strange, and Luke drew back on instinct. He became hyperaware of the sloshing of his bottle. Charlie let out a long sigh and looked away again.

"Just stop Luke. Please. You're just gonna sit there—you're gonna sit there and bitch and moan about this bus and it doesn't matter. Luke, it doesn't matter. Nothin's ever coming." He paused for a moment, face once again tired and sour and sad. "So you might as well shut your mouth." His next pause was longer but he finally spoke. "You're dead." His voice was soft, somehow final.

"What?" Luke said, confused by his friend snapping at him for seemingly no reason. Angry too that it was for some weird story, some unbelievable lie.

"You're *dead*," he said again, emphasizing the two words carefully. "There's nothing left. It's over."

"The fuck are you saying?" said Luke, bottle a few inches from his mouth, now frozen in the air. The thinnest thread of fear was worming its way into the fabric of his mind.

"I'm saying the bus is never coming. There's no bus to come. We're not alive anymore Luke—we're dead."

"What?"

Charlie ran his hands through his hair and Luke noticed his friend's fingers flexing in frustration. "Does the day seem weird to you at all? When did we get to the bus stop? Where are we even going? And the season... It's been getting colder and you haven't noticed. It's been weeks Luke! Weeks." The buzzing of the flies in Luke's ears had faded. He had forgotten to lower his arm and his soda bottle still hovered near his mouth. Charlie began speaking again, softer now. "We have this conversation every single day," he said, sounding profoundly weary. "The seasons are changing. It was August when we died and now October is breathing down our necks. By Christmas we'll be gone. Faded away." He finally looked at his friend, looked him in the eye, and the mixture of sadness and desperation caused Luke's breath to catch. "And I hope to God you remember that you're dead by then, cause I don't want to watch you fall apart and not know what's happening. I don't want to have to hear you scream."

Luke just blinked at him, disbelieving. "Weeks?"

"Yeah. Weeks. You never remember." Charlie scratched the back of his neck. "I remember. I've accepted that we're dead. I think."

"What the fuck happened?"

Charlie choked out a harsh laugh. "Bus crash. Great, right? Why do you think we're here? Don't know what caused it—the driver was sick or distracted or whatever. Can't really read a coroner's report when you're haunting a bus stop. He careened off course, smashed into us. We were sitting right here, just waiting for the bus."

"Did he die?"

"Yeah, I think so." Charlie glanced over his shoulder at a withering wreath of flowers that Luke had somehow missed before. It was the sort of tribute you left when someone died in a car crash. Luke knew there was no one around to leave a tribute for him, not if Charlie was dead. The same went for Charlie but in reverse. Luke felt a sudden bolt of anger.

"Then where the fuck is his ghost?! Why does he get off scot-free?!"

"Maybe he's haunting somewhere else. Maybe he died before he crashed of something natural, and natural causes don't get ghosts. Maybe the universe saves on space that way."

Luke thought about throwing his soda down, about stomping out of the bus stop, but if Charlie was right and this had been happening for weeks maybe he'd already done that. Clearly nothing had come of it. He could still hear the weeping in the graveyard behind him.

"So what are we supposed to do?"

"I dunno. Sit here. Wait. Like I said, by Christmas we'll be gone."

"What makes you so sure about that?" Luke tried to keep his rising irritation and fear out of his voice. No point in alienating the only other person who would be keeping him company for the foreseeable future.

Charlie shrugged. "I dunno. I just know that much. Somehow."

"So we're just..." Luke trailed off and almost left the thought hanging. Instead he forced himself to finish. "Dead.

Charlie just grunted, abandoning the spoken word entirely. He was staring off into the distance again and Luke couldn't help but feel slightly abandoned. It wasn't his fault he kept forgetting, that this conversation was likely tired for his friend.

Luke joined him in staring silently, blankly considering the strip mall across the street. Half the stores were gone, long empty. He saw a gull swooping low over some dumpster. People were still crying behind him, softer now. "Dead," he said again, thoughtfully. Charlie didn't bother to respond. Finally Luke raised the lip of his bottle to his mouth and swallowed the last of his warm soda in a single, greedy gulp. At the sound Charlie turned to look at him and the glint in his eye was a mixture of desperation and excitement. He licked his lips and spoke.

"You never finished your soda before."

WHERE IT ALL STARTED
K. Trap Jones

K. Trap Jones is an author of horror novels and short stories. With inspiration from Dante Alighieri and Edgar Allan Poe, he has a temptation towards narrative folklore, classic literary works and obscure segments within society. His novel *The Sinner* (Blood Bound Books) won the 2010 Royal Palm Literary Award. Other novels include *The Drunken Exorcist* (Necro Publications), *The Harvester* (Blood Bound Books), *One Bad Fur Day* (Sirens Call Publications) and his short story collection *The Crossroads* (Hazardous Press). He is also a member of the Horror Writers Association and can be found lurking around Tampa, Florida. For more on K. Trap Jones visit ktrapjones.wordpress.com.

I heard many folklore tales as I was growing up and I believed every single one of them. The thoughts about witches and monsters all plagued my young mind. The details burned my eyes while I tried desperately to sleep. From mischievous gremlins to a roaming horde of the undead, the stories became tattooed on my mind and infected the thoughts that construct it. With all of the history and fear regarding folklore, how on earth do I find myself in this situation? I am losing grip with reality and not understanding the truth behind the events that unfolded. Folklore is supposed to be something from the past; it is not supposed to be constructed within the present. Unfortunately, I believe that I have done just that. A new folklore has spread through the town and across the mountain. It is one that haunts and disturbs even the older generation; one that involves me. It all started when a reporter stepped foot on my land.

My childhood was filled with lies and deception. No one ever believed that the folklore stories were true, but I saw the demons lurking behind the trees at night. I witnessed the sacrificial pits of the witches as they roasted their victims. I told everyone, but still no one cared. I even showed them the smoldering pits, but they brushed it off as campfires. A wild imagination was what they diagnosed me with, but I knew better. Every night I watched the fires burn. Every morning I saw the half-eaten carcasses buried in shallow graves. I wrote down everything that I experienced within a diary. The other kids called me crazy when I tried to warn them and I was even suspended from school for hanging up the posters. Sure, they were graphic in content, but fear was needed in order for people to take me serious. None of it helped with my popularity, but I didn't care about such frivolous things like that. Especially when I had to prepare for the full moon that was about to happen.

In my mind, there are reasons why folklore exists. It is a warning; a twisted tale that shows evidence of the unexplainable. The stories may be butchered along the way as it is passed through towns, but the core is still there and that is the most important part. If a person can decipher through the fictitious adjectives that are added, then they can truly understand the warning and act appropriately. I had a gift; not many others shared the same. I began to despise those who did not have the same gift.

The house in which I live is isolated on the mountain. A tourist town is a few miles down into the valley. People come here for the river rapids and the beauty of nature, but they don't realize what really lurks in the shadows of the trees. I did not make up these stories; they were passed down through the generations. I know them well; every word flows through my veins as if they are a part of my soul.

Five generations of my family grew up in this house. As a young child, I remember sitting on my great grandfather's lap as he told me stories. I was mesmerized by his words as he puffed on a cigar. He would tell me about the witches and the undead that rise at night. I never had to worry though; he always ended the stories by saying that I was always safe because I was a part of the mountain.

Many years later, I remain the only one from the blood line left. The heritage that flows through the house is a constant reminder of where I came from and those that have passed. The stories all faded over time until a lone man knocked on the door. I was hesitant at first because we were always told to hide when a stranger knocked on the door, but I was no longer that scared little boy anymore. After looking through the window, I saw a skinny man who seemed anxious. My mother always told me to never open the front door to strangers, but I never listened to her anyways.

"Can I help you?" I said through the slightly opened door.

"Are you Jamieson?" the man nervously responded.

My silence was enough of an answer for him to continue.

"My name is Steven Lebout and I work for *The Sentinel.*"

I must have had a confused look or something because he felt the need to clarify.

"It's the local newspaper. I'm doing a story on mountain folklore for the fall issue. Do you mind if I ask you a few questions? I promise that I won't take up too much of your time."

I already broke Rule #1 by not hiding and Rule #2 by answering the door. My father would've been disappointed in me for breaking Rule #3 as I opened the door and allowed the man to enter.

"Thank you in advance for your time. I just have a few questions," he said, looking around the living room.

"Not too many people come up here," I said nervously.

"Can you really blame them? With all the stories that surround this mountain. I'm hoping to clear up some misconceptions, kind of find out why all the myths exist."

"Myths exist for a reason."

"And what reason would that be," he replied, pulling out a small tape recorder. "Do you mind? I am horrible with taking notes."

"I, I...that's alright, I guess."

He was making me nervous and I realized why Rule #1 and Rule #2 were at the top of the list. His eyes roamed every photo on the mantle.

"You come from a large family," he said, taking pictures of the framed photos with a camera.

"Yes, my family has lived here for a long time. What is it that I can help you with?" I said, trying to hurry him up.

"The folklore of the mountain. The deaths and countless missing people throughout the decades; *Death Mountain* is what they call this place now. Doesn't that bother you? Living all by yourself?"

"No, I have outgrown the stories."

"I heard that you were quite the researcher back in the day. Did you find anything interesting that you think would help with the story that I am writing?"

He never looked me in the eye when he spoke. His head never stopped turning around as he scoured the living room.

"What exactly are you looking for?"

"Let me be honest here, I am like you. I believe the stories. I don't think that they are just tall tales spoken through the mouths of children. I believe they actually happened; everything happens for a reason, don't you agree?"

Rule #4 was to never trust anyone, but he seemed reasonable and we shared common interests.

"It's the meaning of the folklore that is the most important," I said.

"Exactly," the man replied. "Most don't understand that."

It was refreshing to hear that response. Every time I said that to someone, they either threw rocks at me or told me to shut up.

"The meaning of folklore gets twisted every time it is passed down, but the core is where the true story exists."

"Of course, and that is why I am here. I need to track the folklore back to the core of the story. Your family has lived on the mountain for so long that I figured what better source of the folklore than here."

I never looked at it that way before. The stories that my great grandfather told me had to be very close to the source of the stories. I could only imagine what his father told him.

"Did you by chance keep any of your research?"

"Yes, I have everything, but it's packed away."

"I would love to see that. It would really help with the story."

"I…I."

"I just thought since we were so similar in our understanding of folklore that we could share the research together."

I started to feel weird because I had just met him, but already saw him as a friend. It had been a long time, actually never, since I had a friend. As my hand turned the cellar door, I knew that I was breaking Rule #5: Never go into the cellar.

A dangling light bulb guided us down the steps. His camera didn't stop flashing. He took so many pictures that I had to actually squint my eyes.

"I hope you don't mind, but my short term memory is not like it was," he said.

"I guess not, but I don't know exactly where the box is. I actually have never been down here before."

"Why not?"

"I was never allowed."

"It's alright. I will help you look."

Through walls of boxes we looked. It felt good to have a friend who shared a common interest. Someone like me didn't have friends. Growing up, it seemed like everyone I met would never come back. My family was all that I had. The mental conversation that I was having with myself didn't last long as it was interrupted by laughter.

"Goldmine!" he said, holding two frames.

"Did you find my journal?" I replied.

"Better than that."

I reached to stop the swinging light bulb. He was taking photos of the frames. The flash kept blinding me to where I couldn't make out the pictures.

"I better get a pay raise. My editor is going to go through the roof when she sees this."

He shuffled through the frames like a deck of cards. I picked up one of the discarded ones and held it up to the light. The grainy black and white photo showed a crowd of people around a fire pit. People were tied to the ground; their corpses were ablaze. Others were standing around. Another photo showed a closer image. I recognized my father, mother and grandfather. My mother was holding me in her arms. Another photo showed my father digging graves.

The shadows of the cellar shifted uncontrollably and made me sick to my stomach. The flashes from the camera blistered my eyes as I stumbled to stay afoot. His laughter dug its way into the core of my skull. Tears flowed down my face. Everything from my youth came back to haunt me. I remembered the fires; I loved to roast marshmallows. I remembered the graves; I played with my cars in them. I buckled over and vomited.

"This will be the story of the year; I'm thinking award," he continued, taking more photos.

Wiping the bile from my chin, I picked up a frame with a family portrait in it. The word *Family* was etched in the hardened wood that constructed the frame. Underneath a work bench, covered in dirt, I saw a corner of a book.

"I hope the camera battery holds up."

From a pile of grime, I pulled out my diary. Worn out through the years, the pages were almost stuck together. Everything was there; my research, my drawings. My eyes swelled with tears as I related the research to my family. It all made sense. The stories were all true, but I was too young to see it at the time. Generation after generation constructed the tales that flowed down the valley. The research within my diary was not enough; everything that was true existed in the one place that I was not allowed to go.

"The glare from the glass is not helping. We need to take the photos out."

The room would not stop spinning. The dust filled my lungs and suffocated my thoughts. The anxiety from the revelation punished my innocence to where I was hearing voices.

You have to deal with this now.

I quickly looked around the cellar for the source of the voice, but saw only darkness.

The family must be protected.

I started to hyperventilate as I reached up to the workbench for support.

You are the only one left.

"Can I take a few of these photos with me?" the reporter said.

He cannot be allowed to leave.

I remember seeing the glistening of the hammer as it fell to the ground before me. The sweat and dirt on my palm suctioned against the handle.

Our family will die.

I saw my reflection in the metal as the camera flash continue to fight the darkness.

No matter what happens, you will always be safe.

In a matter of hours, I had broken every rule that my family lived by, but as that hammer smashed against the skull of the reporter, I felt at peace. It felt as if I had faced the demons that had poisoned my mind for so many years. I carefully placed all of the frames back into the boxes before dragging the reporter up the stairs. He didn't wake up until much later when he was staked to the ground over a pile of logs. His words meant nothing to me as he was no longer my friend. The camera and recorder rested on his chest as lighter fluid saturated his shirt. I sat reading my diary; all the words that twisted reality into folklore. It was like reading a fictional story that was actually real. It was all that I needed in order to continue the tale; to continue the legacy that my family had started.

The stars were bright that night. There was a calming breeze that rustled the trees and whispered the rules into my ears once again. I felt my father watching me from the trees and my mother guiding me from the sky. I heard my grandfather in the wind, letting me know that I would always be safe. My family was the foundation of folklore. I was not about to be the one to let the story die.

FAIRBORN, OHIO
WHERE TRAINS AND GHOSTS STILL RUN
Kerry G.S. Lipp

Kerry teaches English at a community college by evening and writes horrible things by night. He hates the sun. His parents started reading his stories and now he's out of the will. Kerry's work appears in several anthologies including *DOA2* from Blood Bound Books and *Attack of the B-Movie Monsters* from Grinning Skull Press. His story *Smoke* pioneered The Wicked Library podcast's explicit content warning. Currently, he's shopping a bizarro novella and editing his first novel. KGSL blogs at HorrorTree.com and will launch his own website newworldhorror.com sometime before he dies.

Fairborn, Ohio lies on the north side of Dayton. It's the kind of place where you won't get murdered, but you might get your ass kicked. It's a crossroads. It's one of few places where railroad tracks and airline trajectory constantly intersect. Fairborn surrounds Wright Patterson Air Force Base and many believe that the base is the only thing keeping Fairborn alive. While probably true, Fairborn is as real as any other small city. The railroad tracks, which even in 2012 are constantly rumbling, and the skies shake with the scream of passing planes. On Main Street there are still used book stores, comic book shops, stores dedicated to Halloween year round, locally owned restaurants and even a five and dime.

Though the city is urbanized, there are still skeletons of long forsaken stores, trees to climb, bridges to build forts under, and wilderness to explore. This story begins with two boys exploring such wilderness and not what they happened to find, but what happened to find them.

Davie and Jared chattered, each holding a brown paper sack that held the newest issue of *Locke & Key* as they left The Bookery comic store. Summer was winding down and school was getting ready to start. They had one last weekend of freedom and they intended to stretch it out until that final minute when that first bell rang. Though neither would admit it, they were both excited and a little tense about starting high school. They were both a couple of nobodies, but everyone is until they walk through the front doors of that high school. They could see a massive change on that sun-setting horizon and were dragging their feet as the sun and the summer and their childhood, like a jet overhead, rapidly approached its final descent.

"OK," Davie said, "We'll each run home, grab our stuff and then we'll meet at the train."

"We should've just brought our stuff with us," Jared whined. "Then we could just go get to reading. It's gonna be dark soon."

"That's the whole point. Who the hell reads *Locke and Key* anywhere but the dark? C'mon Jared, we've got it perfect. That's what the flashlights are for. Quit being a baby."

"But…"

"Plus," Davie cut him off. "I've got some cool stuff to help us celebrate the end of summer. Stuff that I wouldn't dare carry with me on Main Street!"

"Uh…Stuff? Like what?"

"Grown up stuff. High school stuff. I think it'll be a perfect way to close out the summer, and we both know that no one ever comes out to the train. We can read and do whatever we want in peace."

"What other things?" Jared asked as he kicked a rock into a pothole.

"Surprises. I'll meet you at the train in thirty."

The sun bled in a widespread smatter of radiant pink as the boys parted ways on the corner of Main Street and Central Avenue.

***

Even though he'd acted tough in front of Jared, Davie was anxious about what was going to happen. His older brother had been home from college for a good chunk of the summer, and Davie had gotten pretty good at exploring his bedroom. Davie could do it without getting caught, or at least he thought so. Phil had never said anything.

His older brother's room was like a decadent Mecca of porno magazines, cigarettes, comics, horror novels and marijuana. Davie used all these over the summer, and had slowly been pinching bits of marijuana as a way for him and Jared to say goodbye to the summer: A rite of passage that might make them a little cooler when they hit high school. And just a little cooler could be the difference between life and death as a Fairborn Skyhawk.

Davie's nerves rattled with excitement. A brand new issue of *Locke and Key*, some weed, some smokes and the train, he and Jared's secret spot for years. He'd always heard his brother and the older kids talk about how much cooler weed made stuff like movies. He thought it would be a perfect fit for a dark comic book.

He stuffed his lighter and his flashlight and everything else into his backpack, slipped his arms through the straps and while the butterflies in his stomach beat their wings, he beat his feet across the street, through the park, down the hill and straight to the train.

Jared was already there, sitting on top of the train looking out, a sinister grin splitting his face as the sun faded to a dusky purple ember. Cars zoomed across the nearby overpass and faraway lights provided the only light as the moon and the stars traded places with the sun.

Davie looked at the tall abandoned train car, white paint chipped like lost snowflakes and more primer than anything, it sat long forgotten, orphaned in what they called the train yard graveyard.

"Tim Waggoner," Jared shouted from atop the train. Their favorite game. One would start a category, either athletes or actors or bands tied to Ohio. You had to name one back to keep the game going. If you repeated a name or paused too long, you lost.

"Gary Braunbeck," Davie said climbing up to the top of the train.

"Katrina Kittle," Jared countered.

"How about someone that hasn't taught at Sinclair for Christ's sake. It's a big state."

"Still your turn."

"Bleh. Brady Allen."

"Good one. I like him. I'd love to see what he'd come up with if we showed him the train yard graveyard."

"Quit stalling."

"R.L. Stine."

"Nice. *Fear Street*. Christopher Moore."

"Marilyn Manson."

"Oh that's bullshit."

"*Long Hard Road Out of Hell*. Look it up."

"Yeah, I know but…"

"Ambrose Bierce," said a voice. They were too into the game to have noticed him. They jumped at the sound of his voice and looked down at him standing a few yards away walking on the half mile stretch of train track that no longer connected to anything.

It was twilight but he seemed to glow, transparent yet radiant, like a specter. He smiled at them and removed his battered baseball cap, dark red with a letter C smeared with grime and dirt. His clothes were old and dirty but intact and his smile was genuine. A quick glance into his eyes revealed the deepest and most sincere sadness either boy had ever seen. The man shifted in his dusty boots and rocks crunched underfoot.

"Your turn," he said.

They boys both stared, frozen, looking at this man who had just joined their game. They'd been coming to the train yard graveyard for years now and had never seen a soul.

Who was this guy?

93

"The Owl Bridge dude right?" Davie asked.

The man nodded, "Your turn."

Alone at dusk, sitting on top of the train with this stranger standing below them, the boys should've been terrified, but the stranger wasn't scary. That was the crazy part. He was friendly and sad. Both boys stood and looked at each other.

"I think he's fine," Davie whispered. "Let's talk to him. And then he'll go away. If we ignore him, he might get mad."

"Fine," Jared grumbled.

"You kinda scared us mister. We lost our train of thought. Guess you win this round."

The man smiled.

"I guess I'll take the win," he said, gesturing to the boys, looking for their names.

"I'm Davie and this is Jared," Davie said.

"Paulie McDonald," he said. "Nice to meet you."

"Yeah, you too Mr. McDonald," Davie said, hesitant, captivated by the man's glow.

"I like your game. It's nice that you guys are so proud of where you come from. A lot of good things besides college football come out of Ohio. Glad to see people that appreciate them."

"Thank you sir," Davie said.

"I noticed you guys got a thing for horror writers. You named a few that most people may not even know. Although they should. Some fine writers you boys named."

"Who are you Mr. McDonald?" Davie asked.

"Well, since you boys like horror stories, I'll tell you mine."

They nodded, fear forgotten. Only interest lit their faces, and it made them glow like the apparition in front of them.

"Like most stories do," McDonald said, "It starts with a woman and a bad decision."

McDonald paused, "I reckon you boys don't have a lot of experience with women yet, and that's OK. There's no rush, take it from me. But this is my story of me and a woman that I loved. I thought she loved me too, but as you'll see, I was wrong. Her name was Ginger."

"Tell us," Davie said.

"Me and Ginger were young and in love and this must've been fifty or so years ago. It's hard to keep track boys. Anyway, we really got on but we were thrill seekers and we were poor. Thrills and poverty are a bad combination. What that meant was that we weren't scared to steal. We enjoyed the process, the heist and we liked filling our bellies. Though we loved the thrill, neither one of us had the kill. At least I didn't think so until that bank job went bad."

Only a few seconds into the story and the boy's had forgotten all about their comics.

"We always used guns. People react faster and are much more willing to do what you say when you've got a gun. So we used them, but we agreed that we'd never fire. She broke that promise. A job went a little crazy, but I think we could've made it out. She didn't, and she started shooting. Left me with no choice but to start shooting myself, and when it was all finished, four people were dead and several wounded. But we got away, took a nice chunk of cash too."

Davie poked Jared with his bony elbow. They looked at each other, faces aghast. They knew this story. But they weren't scared of McDonald. He was calm and nice, and they knew that he was dead. They knew how this story ended.

"I can see by your faces that you know where this story is going."

"Yes sir. We've heard this one a few times."

"Well, let me finish with my side. We'll see how it lines up."

They nodded.

"I didn't have a problem stealing, loved the rush, but I wasn't a killer. And she made me one. I told her that we were done after that. No more robbing. I couldn't handle it and we had to hide. We were looking at the death penalty.

"Ginger agreed. Constantly apologizing. She said she couldn't get over the guilt and I didn't think that I could either. We didn't spend the money and we didn't rob again. We hid out and ate cheap for weeks. We were all busted up. I told her that I couldn't keep living like this, and she agreed.

"We talked things over and we decided on a suicide pact. You boys know what that is?"

They nodded.

"She told me that she'd anonymously donate the money to charity, and then we'd die together. And we were supposed to. We set the day, checked the train schedule and set the time. We were both all ate up with guilt and saw no other way out. We'd die making love on the train tracks.

"Ginger told me she wanted to be on top, and I liked her that way. We wrote notes apologizing, got right with God, and slowly we started to make love in the middle of the afternoon before the train came by. When we started to feel the rails vibrate beneath us our pace quickened and when the train came into sight, we both cried and said that we loved each other.

"And then, she took my head in both her hands and kissed me. I thought we were going to die that way, but instead she broke the kiss and started smashing my head into the ground until I passed out. Then she jumped up and ran away. I know she didn't turn around to watch, but I know she paused her stride when the train whistle blew and she heard it hit my limp body.

"I can't say for sure why she did it, but I think she never took that money to charity, and I don't think she felt bad at all about killing those people. I think she killed me too, so she could move on and leave me behind. She didn't love me. She loved the money, the thrill, and now that she'd had a taste, the kill too."

The boys were silent.

"So here I am. I've been wandering these tracks for years, hoping that she'll come back or that they'll reconnect these broken ones so I can walk a little farther and look around. Ain't much to see in this little stretch."

"Jesus," Davie said. "That's a story Mr. McDonald. I'm so sorry. Is there anything we can do to help you?"

"I hoped you'd ask that," McDonald said. "I think you boys could help me out quite a bit."

"How?"

"Well I know you ain't railroad workers, but I expect that if you could build me a path to the main tracks, I could cover more ground. I don't know why, but I can only walk on the railroad tracks. This stretch here isn't taking me nowhere, and I'm sick of wandering it. You boys think you could build me a bridge to the main ones? I don't expect to find Ginger, but I'd like to keep looking, and though I like this area, I'm ready for a change of scenery."

Davie looked at Jared, and at the comics and booze and marijuana forgotten; they would help Paulie McDonald.

"I think you boys can do it with branches and sticks and not railroad ties. At least I hope so, or I'm stuck here forever."

Davie and Jared collected sticks and stones and whatever else they could find and built a shoddy path that resembled railroad tracks. In the end it led from the train yard graveyard up to the mainline.

Paulie McDonald followed them the whole way. It worked.

When it was finished, McDonald stood at a new crossroads and tried to decide which direction to head. They said their goodbyes.

"You think you'll find her?" Davie asked.

"I doubt it," McDonald said, "But I hope I find something. Thank you both for listening and helping an old ghost."

The boys nodded and McDonald adjusted his Reds baseball cap and gave them an informal salute. Then he picked a direction and started walking. His strides were long and slow and full of purpose.

Davie and Jared looked at each other.

McDonald didn't look back.

THE CRAWLING MAN
Sean Logan

Sean Logan's stories have appeared in more than thirty publications, including *Black Static, Penumbra, Supernatural Tales, The New Gothic* and *Dark Visions*. He lives in northern California in a little house with a big, scary Rottweiler that will run and hide at the first sign of trouble.

Let's just skip the part of the story where I tell you this is all true. It *is* true, and I know it's true—every word of it—but I'm not going to try to convince you. First of all, you wouldn't believe me. Second, it doesn't really matter. So go right ahead and be as skeptical as you like. I don't mind.

So with that out of the way, I'll begin—

This all started in my seventh grade English class. It was a slow Monday morning, and the students were still getting back up to speed after the weekend, slouching lazily at their desks, barely paying attention to my lesson. However, throughout the period, I kept noticing that one student in the back of the room looked troubled, a boy named Randal Milman who was about a foot taller and twenty pounds lighter than any other boy in class. He was fidgeting, chewing his cuticles, stealing quick furtive glances behind him and out the window, like he was anticipating something unpleasant creeping up behind him. Was he worried that one of the other boys would sneak up and flick him on the ear? He was often picked on. But no, it was nothing so trivial. His dark, red-rimmed eyes suggested a more serious threat than some childish shenanigans.

When the bell rang and the students ambled out of class, I asked Randal to stay after. I had spoken to him before. He had once confided in me that he was having a hard time at home, so I would check in with him from time to time to see how he was doing. He lived in a small farm house at the end of Occidental Road with a father who was...well, let's just say his father was not a very nice man. So I asked Randal if there was a problem.

"No," he said, "everything's fine," but even as he said this, I saw his eyes begin to shimmer.

"What is it?" I asked. "Is it your father? Did he hurt you?"

"No," he said, "it's nothing like that." He looked around to see if we were alone, and then he leaned in close to me. "Can I trust you? If I tell you something, will you keep it between us?"

"Of course," I said. "You can tell me anything. I mean that."

He took a deep breath and let it out slowly, then said, "What do you think of curses? Like, do you think that's a real thing? Do you think people can be cursed?"

I nearly laughed when he said this, but from his rigid expression I could tell he believed it. "I don't know," I said. "I mean, no. No, I don't think a person can have a curse on them. Good or bad luck, maybe. A little bit. But not a curse."

Randal turned his wide, haunted eyes directly to mine. "They are real," he said. "I'm cursed."

I tried to laugh lightly, deflect the impact of his words. "I'm sure that's not true," I told him, "but tell me what happened. Why do you think you're cursed?"

"It was a story," he said. "I'm cursed because of a story I was told."

This was absurd, of course, but I wanted to be supportive. I just nodded and listened as Randal told me what happened.

He said that he had gone camping that past weekend with his friend Paulo. Late on Saturday night, after the hot dogs had been eaten, the s'mores had been reduced to a few sticky spots on their fingers and jeans, and after Paulo's father had gone to bed, the two of them stayed up, watching the glowing embers of the campfire, feeling its warmth in front of them and the cold night air at their backs. It was then that Paulo told Randal that a few days earlier he had read a story—and that it was not like other stories. He got it from his grandmother. Randal himself had never met her; he only knew what Paulo told him, that she was a fiery gray-haired woman who lived alone in an old moldering house in the woods, isolated from the neighbors, who thought the house to be haunted. She was an outcast in their family, but Paulo went to visit her occasionally. He didn't say much else about her, but he mentioned that she sometimes performed strange rituals, chanting words that weren't English. She had a room filled with dried insects and roots and powders. And shelves full of old books. One book she kept in a wooden box on a high shelf. Knowing this book must be important, Paulo sneaked into her room to read it.

The book, he said, looked like it was covered with leather, but when he touched it he felt certain it was bound in human skin. With an excited chill in his blood, Paulo sat the book on the dirty wooden floor and read the story within.

Just as he finished the tale, his grandmother came into the room and caught him in the act. Her eyes flared and her lips pulled tight in a grimace.

Paulo cowered, but her expression relaxed. She sat down next to him and told him that he must never tell that story to another person. Because if he did, the Crawling Man would come.

Of course, Paulo was intrigued and disturbed by this, but his grandmother wouldn't explain. She would only say that if you saw the Crawling Man, you'd be dead within days.

With those words, the two boys sat quietly by the fire for a moment. Then Paulo spoke, "So how about I tell you that story?" he said. "Let's see what happens."

Randal knew this was all silly. Stories can't hurt you. Just hearing a story won't make bad things happen. Randal knew this. But still he felt a sickening sense of dread at the notion. He pretended he just wasn't interested in hearing the story, but Paulo dared him. "I'm too tired," he said, but Paulo double dared him, and Randal acquiesced. Quietly, under a clear, star-filled sky, Paulo told Randal the story from his grandmother's book.

At this point, I asked Randal about the story, what was the tale his friend told him, but he refused to say. If he did, he said, I would suffer the same curse.

He continued, telling me that after the story he crawled into his tent, slipped into the cool soft folds of his sleeping bag and lay quietly listening to the crackling of the dying fire. His friend Paulo was soon asleep, and as he began to drift off as well, he heard the snapping of a branch. There was a rustling in the brush nearby. It must be an animal, he thought. A raccoon. He grabbed the flashlight from his backpack and aimed it outside the tent at a copse of young pine trees beside their camp. He flicked the flashlight on and there at the end of the bright white beam was a man crawling through the dirt. He was pale white and his eyes were glassy black like balls of onyx. And worst of all, his head was twisted around in the wrong direction, so his chin pointed up toward the moon, and his hair hung down like a strange beard.

When Randal saw this, he gasped and lurched backward, and the man crawled off into the woods, crawling as fast as a man can run.

The rest of that sleepless night and the next day, Randal didn't speak of what he saw to his friend or his friend's father. He could not have seen what he had seen. It could only have been a dream. Paulo's story had frightened him and induced a nightmare that just felt real. Terribly, terribly real.

Randal returned home to his farm house. It was small with only two bedrooms. Randal's father slept in one, and his half-mad grandfather occupied the other, so Randal slept in the attic. It was not so bad, he said. The ceiling was low and slanted on both sides of the room, but it was big enough for a single bed and a desk and there was a window that looked out over the apple orchard to the east.

When Randal went to bed that night he had a nervous prickling at his skin like it was crawling with insects, but he tried to convince himself that what he had seen the night before wasn't real. There was nothing to be afraid of. He didn't quite believe this, but that is what he told himself as he turned off his bedside lamp and got into bed. It was another clear, bright night and Randal could see the full moon shinning in through the window to his attic room.

After some time, the invisible insects on his skin stopped crawling and the knotted muscles in his shoulders began to loosen. Maybe it was true. Maybe what he'd seen the night before was just a dream after all. But once again, as his mind began to wander into sleep, he was snapped out of his near-slumber by a noise. Something was scraping through the dirt and gravel path that lead to the front of the house. He heard a hollow thumping up the steps and across the creaking wood of the porch.

Randal lay in the dark with an oppressive sense of dread, his heart beginning to beat heavily, praying he wouldn't hear a knock. But he did, a slow rapping on the front door that echoed through his quiet house.

Randal didn't move. If this visitor at his door was so important, his father could answer it.

Three more slow, heavy knocks.

His father wasn't answering. He had probably had too much to drink and his grandfather was too old and senile to hear. Randal should probably answer it, but he felt frozen and immobile, petrified there in his bedsheets.

Three more knocks, but this time it wasn't a knock on the door, but on the side of the house. It almost sounded as if someone was knocking on the wall *above* the door.

There was no way Randal would answer it. He would just wait until they went away and whoever it was could come back tomorrow.

The knocking continued, heavier and more insistent than before and higher up the side of the house, well above the door.

Randal pulled the covers over his head, a tremor passing through him like the chill of a fever.

Whoever it was outside Randal's house was not merely knocking but pounding against the wall, still higher. They must be on a ladder. It was far too high for a person to reach.

Randal considered looking out his window, but the thought of what he might see numbed him with terror.

Bang. Bang. Bang. The pounding continued, and now it was just below the window to Randal's attic room.

The light of the moon seemed to go dark for a moment. Randal turned to the window, and there he was—the Crawling Man, scurrying across the glass, fifteen feet above the ground. The pale man stopped midway across the window and turned his twisted head toward Randal. He glared at Randal with his big black eyes, his mouth pulled down at the corners in a severe frown, but with his head turned backward, it looked like an evil grin, and Randal saw that his teeth were as sharp and jagged as the teeth of a shark.

Randal screamed then, but no one came, not his drunk father nor his insane grandfather. Poor Randal pulled the covers back over his head and screamed until his throat was ragged and sore.

And that was the end of his story. I now realized that he looked tired because he had not slept in two days. And the fact that he looked scared—well, of course he did! He had undergone a terrible ordeal. I didn't believe that any of this was real—I certainly didn't think he had seen an actual person crawling on his second story window—but he was clearly upset and had imagined something so dreadful he was unable to sleep.

"I'm so sorry you've gone through this," I said. "I think the story your friend told you and the fact that you haven't slept is making you imagine terrible things."

Randal protested. "No," he said. "No, it's all real! I saw the Crawling Man. And the next time I see him is not going to be on my window. It's going to be *inside* my house—inside my room!"

I told him that he was getting himself worked up over nothing. He should tell his father he couldn't sleep and see if he would give him a sleeping pill. One good night's sleep and he'll be as good as new in the morning.

"But I can't sleep," he said. "What if he comes while I'm asleep? What if I can't wake up? I won't be able to stop him."

"Trust me," I said, "you have nothing to worry about. I know you're scared and I don't blame you a bit. But what you're seeing isn't real. There is no Crawling Man and there is no curse. The story you heard was just a story. You've got an active imagination. It will serve you well one day—who knows, maybe you'll write scary stories yourself when you get older. But right now, that imagination of yours is making you crazy. So do as I say: go home, get some sleep, and I'll see you right back here tomorrow. And I bet that when I do, you'll be a whole different person."

Randal agreed to take my advice, but when he walked away, he was slouching and his head sagged. He looked like he was walking toward his own execution. Before he left the classroom, he turned back and gave me one last look. I'll never forget the expression that clouded his face. His furrowed brow displayed the fear he no doubt felt, but there was another quality to his countenance. It was almost a look of guilt, though I couldn't imagine what he would have to feel guilty about. I wouldn't be able to ask him later, because that was the last time I ever saw him.

The next day when I pulled into the faculty parking lot and was getting out of my car, the principal came out to meet me. He told me that Randal

Milman had been found dead that morning by his grandfather. His neck had been broken. The police brought Randal's father in for questioning, but he was released later that afternoon. There was no evidence he had done this terrible thing. There were no clues at all to tell them what had happened. Randal's father had said the only thing out of the ordinary had been that the previous night he thought he'd heard Randal crawling around his room. This struck him as strange because he was surprised his son was up and about—he had given him a sleeping pill before bed.

There was one more detail the principal told me about Randal's death: when they found him, his head had been twisted all the way around.

***

Earlier I had said that I knew the story Randal told me was true. Since I wasn't there, you might wonder how I could be so sure. I know, because last night the Crawling Man came to *me*. I saw him creeping across the grass in my back yard like a giant white spider. I looked down from my bedroom window into its big black eyes, and I saw that it was Randal Milman, with his head twisted backward. The Crawling Man had gotten him, and he had *become* the Crawling Man.

When I saw him, I realized his story was true—he had been cursed, and now *I* was cursed. It all started for Randal because his friend had told him a story. What I now understood was that the story he had been told was the story of the Crawling Man. And that was the story he told to me. He knew he was doomed, that he was going to become the Crawling Man. He might be trapped in that pale, broken form for years, for centuries until someone else received the curse. So he told the story to me. So that I would replace him. And in a matter of days I will.

***

You'll remember that when I began this tale, I told you it didn't matter whether or not you believed it was true. Go ahead and be skeptical.

It did not matter, because tonight or tomorrow or sometime soon, you will believe.

You see, just like Randal Milman, I don't want to be trapped, crawling through the night with my neck twisted, seeing the world turned upside down. So with these words the story of the Crawling Man has once again been told.

Now tonight, as you lay in bed, listen for the sound of a snapping twig, or rustling leaves, or a banging on your walls. For that will be the sound of the Crawling Man.

And he'll be coming for you.

LOOKING GLASS
David Massengill

David Massengill is the author of *Fragments of a Journal Salvaged from a Charred House in Germany, 1816 and other stories* (Hammer & Anvil Books). Dozens of his short works of literary and horror fiction have appeared in literary journals, including *Burial Day Books, Eclectica Magazine, Word Riot, Pulp Metal Magazine, Yellow Mama,* and *3 A.M. Magazine,* among others. His fiction has also appeared in the anthologies *Gothic Blue Book: The Revenge Edition, State of Horror: California, Long Live the New Flesh: Year Two,* and *Clones, Fairies, & Monsters in the Closet.* His website is davidmassengillfiction.com.

Lou and Charles followed the tour guide out of the low-ceilinged structure that had once served as slave quarters. They entered a courtyard lit by gaslight. Lou whispered to his boyfriend, "This house tour's depressing me. Should we ditch it and try that coffee shop that serves the upside down pineapple cake? I was thinking I could give you your birthday present early." He reached inside a pocket of his denim jacket and touched the card for Charles.

"My birthday's tomorrow," Charles said. "I think I can wait until then. You're acting unusually spontaneous, Mr. Rudson. You're not one to cut a tour or any other planned event short."

Lou wanted to say he was ready to make some changes. He was going to be more flexible and less cautious for the sake of their relationship.

But before he could the tour guide—a plump, white-haired Georgia native in her sixties—addressed the group: "This being Halloween season, the Historic Savannah Twilight Tour has a special treat for y'all. We'll be talking about Southern death and mourning customs while we explore the main house."

Charles grinned and placed a hand on Lou's lower back. He asked, "How could I pass up a lecture on death the night before my 39th birthday?"

As the tour wound its way through the large, stately rooms of the Federal-style house, the tour guide explained why this was the ideal setting for their morbid topic of discussion. The man who'd built the house—

either Jebediah or Jedediah Something, if Lou had heard correctly—died during the Fall of Atlanta in 1864. He'd been visiting friends when the Union troops seized the city. A gang of Northern soldiers dragged him out of his friends' mansion and carved him up with their bayonets. Upon hearing about her husband's death, J. Something's childless wife sold their property and moved into a convent on Tybee Island, where she died from yellow fever at the age of 25.

"This was the husband and wife's bedroom," the tour guide said, "and that was their mirror—also known as their looking glass." She pointed at a large rectangle of black cloth hanging on one wall. It was just above a sign warning DON'T TOUCH PLEASE. Lou noticed the ornate gold frame protruding from the sides and bottom of the cloth. The frame looked chipped in some places and dangerously sharp in others. Lou shivered as he stared at the dark object.

"Back then," the tour guide said, "people would cover a mirror so their deceased loved one's spirit wouldn't get trapped inside." She motioned for the group to accompany her into the hallway. "People would also stop all the clocks at the time of the loved one's death. The grandfather clock out here will show you what time it was when the mistress of this house passed in 1867."

Lou felt Charles's hand on his wrist as the group filtered out of the bedroom. When the couple was alone in the room, Charles motioned toward the open window next to the canopy bed. Lou could see one of Savannah's many historic squares outside. Lamplight illuminated couples sitting closely on benches. He heard a band in a neighboring house playing "Moon River"—a tune, according to Lou's guidebook, penned by Savannah native Johnny Mercer. A man and a woman slow danced near the trunk of a palm tree.

"If you get rid of the black cloth and the gothic floral wallpaper this actually wouldn't be a bad bedroom," Charles said. He glanced around the chamber. "The husband and wife may have had troubled lives, but their home and their marriage became the stuff of historical tours."

Lou suddenly felt self-conscious about his and Charles's relationship. He recalled the fight they'd had some days before their flight from Seattle to Savannah. Charles had once again brought up that they'd been dating for four years and they still weren't living together. They always spent Friday and Saturday nights and two weeknights together, as if their relationship was on a schedule. "I feel like I need a love life that doesn't have these boundaries," Charles said. "And I'm not sure you can truly give yourself to me." Lou gave his usual defense—that being a paralegal at the firm where he worked utterly exhausted him during the week, that their lack of codependency allowed Charles to maintain his many friendships—but he realized these were hardly excuses for them not sharing an apartment.

His real defense was a great and shadowy fear that had a little something to do with his parents divorcing decades ago and Charles possibly telling him one day that he was no longer in love with him.

But Lou never voiced that fear to Charles.

He felt it now, though, as he slipped his hand inside his pocket and fingered the card. Music drifted into the bedroom and Charles's shoulder touched his as they peered through the window. Lou sensed this was the moment to give Charles his birthday present.

But Lou couldn't remove the card. His hand was shaking.

"Come on, y'all." The tour guide poked her head inside the doorway. "The dead don't appreciate folks dilly-dallying in their bedrooms."

"Sorry," Charles said before following her into the hallway.

Lou couldn't move. He was too angry with himself. He'd vowed before this trip that he was going to be more assertive in his and Charles's relationship and stop acting cowardly.

His exasperation made him want to hit or throw something. Instead, he stepped toward the mirror and, ignoring the *DON'T TOUCH PLEASE* sign, yanked off the black cloth. Gripping the material, he had the weird idea he'd torn off a massive scab. When he looked into the mirror he froze.

He had no reflection.

"Hey, dilly-dallier," Charles said.

Lou glanced at his boyfriend, who leaned against a banister.

"We're heading downstairs. We're about to learn why people always carried the dead feet-first out the front door."

Lou looked back at the mirror. He saw his parted blond hair; his pale face, which Charles always called "studious" because of its often-furrowed brow; his green eyes that showed terror.

"What's wrong?" Charles asked. "Did the cloth fall off?"

Lou forced a nod and clumsily draped the black material over the frame. "I'm putting it back right now."

As they lay in their hotel bed a few hours later, Lou kept staring at the same page of his Malcolm Gladwell book, unable to move from one sentence to the next. How could there not have been a reflection? He asked himself once again. Did he just imagine that? Was this some sign of mental illness? At 37, he was surely too young for dementia.

Charles clicked off his bedside lamp and peered at Lou with sleepy eyes. He ran a hand through his curly salt-and-pepper hair. "I'm not sure if I feel like going to that Bonaventure Cemetery tomorrow," he said. "I think I've had enough death for a few days."

Lou set down his book on his bare stomach. Once again, he checked the mirror facing their queen-sized bed. The mirror was on top of a dresser. Thankfully, he saw himself sitting up with his book. He also saw

Charles place a hand on his chest.

"You sure you're all right? You've barely spoken since we left that house." Charles poked one of Lou's ribs and joked, "Maybe you're mad I ordered us the key lime pie instead of the pineapple cake."

"Not at all," Lou said, turning to his boyfriend. "I think I'm still jet-lagged."

"Me, too." Charles offered him a lingering kiss on the lips and then rolled over onto his side. "I'm glad we're here together. I feel closer to you."

The comment gave Lou a momentary sense of ease and allowed him to forget his ridiculous worry about the mirror. He looked past Charles's prone body and saw his boyfriend's leather jacket hanging from the back of a desk chair. Lou had slipped the card inside the pocket while Charles was brushing his teeth. Charles would inevitably discover it before they left for breakfast tomorrow.

"Sleep well," Lou said. He looked at himself once more in the mirror and saw the hint of a smile on his face.

After setting his book on the nightstand, he glanced at the lace window curtains fluttering in the breeze coming from outside. Next to the window was a pleasant framed painting of a steamboat chugging along the Savannah River. Lou felt Charles shift his leg until it settled against his.

Your love life is in order, Lou told himself. And then he turned out the light.

He awoke to the sound of horses' hoofs in the street below their second-story room. The horses slowed and snorted loudly outside the hotel. Lou noticed an oppressive humidity had invaded the space. He cracked open his eyes and looked at the window. The moonlit curtains were motionless. He saw Charles still lay on his side. The digital clock on the nightstand near Charles showed it was just before midnight.

A foul smell suddenly filled the room. There were hints of ash and rot in the odor. Lou wondered if some animal had died beneath a floorboard or on the oak tree outside their window. He was about to leave the bed and sniff outside the window when he saw the man standing at the foot of their mattress.

Lou gasped at the sight.

The stranger wore a top hat, a long black frock coat, and a string-style cravat. His soiled clothing made him look as if he'd been rolling through dirt. His limp brown hair hung to his shoulders. He had glaring dark eyes and slash-like wounds covering his face.

Worst of all, he had no lower jaw. His tongue and shredded cheeks dangled over a thin neck.

Lou sat up, his naked back pressed against the headboard. "Get out of here!" he said, his voice squeaking from his fear.

The stranger didn't move.

Lou frowned when he saw the mirror behind the figure.

It was the looking glass from the house tour. It seemed even larger than before. The black cloth was in place.

A nightmare, Lou told himself. This couldn't actually be happening. "Charles," he said, but his boyfriend remained on his side, breathing steadily.

The man placed a knee of his filthy black trousers on the bed and began to crawl toward Lou, his blood-red tongue nearly touching the comforter.

Lou heard the words of the tour guide: *Those Union soldiers used their bayonets on him like he was a jack-o'-lantern.*

"Charles!" Lou cried. Again, his boyfriend failed to respond. He also didn't move when the man pulled the comforter away from their bodies.

Lou tried to leave the bed, but his limbs were paralyzed. The man wrapped weirdly hot hands around his ankles and dragged him toward the end of the mattress.

"Charles, please," Lou said as his body slid toward the edge.

His boyfriend's arm stirred. Charles reached for the retreating comforter. He pulled the blanket until it covered his shoulder, and then he was still.

Lou's body fell from the bed and hit the hardwood floor.

He no longer felt the man's grip. He was able to move his limbs again, and he kneeled on the floor.

The man had disappeared.

"He wasn't real," Lou whispered, preparing to rise from the floor.

And then he heard a creaking sound. He looked up to see the mirror tipping over from the dresser. It was the mirror from the house, but now it was uncovered. He glimpsed his reflection before the glass shattered over his head.

The heat woke Lou. He was sweating, and he felt something heavy on top of him. His eyes shot open when he recalled the falling mirror and the ghoulish man.

He realized the weight came from a soaked comforter. He pushed the blanket down to his waist. He was relieved to find himself lying in bed.

Last night's horrible events really had just been part of a dream.

He lay on his side, facing the painting of the steamboat. The artwork looked amateurish and faded in the daylight. He saw the window was shut and there was a long, curving crack in its center. Lou sensed it was late morning. He moved one ankle toward Charles's side of the bed, expecting their feet to touch, but there was only mattress.

Lou rolled over. Charles had indeed left the bed. The power must have gone out because the digital clock on Charles's side of the bed was blinking the time *12:00 AM.*

"Charles?" Lou called, expecting a response from the bathroom. "Why'd you shut the window?"

Silence except for the sound of a tour trolley passing outside.

"Handsome? You here?" Lou sat up and saw the bathroom door was ajar and the space was dark. He wondered if Charles had gone downstairs to the hotel's dining room. But he knew they had reservations at that riverside restaurant that supposedly served the best chicken and waffles in all of Georgia.

He felt a twinge of worry when he saw Charles's jacket hanging from the chair and his sneakers on the floor.

He probably brought other shoes, Lou decided. And why would he need a jacket on such a warm morning? Maybe he'd gone out to treat himself to a New Orleans-style iced coffee or take a stroll along that nearby street that was perpetually shaded by Spanish moss. Wanting to join him, Lou left the bed and retrieved a shirt and pair of jeans from his suitcase.

He winced as he put on the pants in front of the mirror.

He saw a reflection of Charles. His boyfriend lay on the bed. His eyes were tearing, and he wore a dreadful expression on his face, as if he weren't on the bed but in some faraway, painful place.

Lou reeled around and saw the bed was empty.

He didn't know what he'd just experienced. His imagination, maybe, or some sort of vision? He didn't care. He only wanted to find his boyfriend. He hurried to Charles's jacket and plunged a hand inside the pocket to check if Charles's wallet was in there.

He found the card instead. On the front of the envelope were the words *open no later than your birthday.*

The envelope was still sealed.

Lou had thought the card was so clever. On the front was an illustration of an alligator with its head partly submerged beneath a black river. Ominous, haunted-looking trees lined the riverbanks.

Inside the card, two smiling gators faced each other. Printed above their heads were the words *THE SWAMP IS HEAVEN WHEN I'M WITH YOU.*

Lower on the card, Lou had written:

Happy Birthday
When we find the right apartment, will you move in with me?
Yours, Lou

Lou tried not to panic after he found Charles's wallet and hotel key card in the other pocket. He immediately called the front desk and asked if they'd seen a 6-foot man with curly black hair this morning.

"There's silver in his hair, too," Lou said, "and he's got a birthmark under his chin that kind of looks like a cloud."

The front desk hadn't seen such a man.

Lou was about to dash out of the room when he heard the faint, distant humming coming from the mirror. The tune was "Moon River," and the shaky voice was Charles's. Lou pressed his hand against the mirror, staring at his lonely, terrified reflection.

His heartbeat quickened when he felt something pressing against the other side of the glass.

"I know you're there," Lou said even though the words sounded crazy. "I'll get to you, Charles. I will."

LOST DAYS
Edward J. McFadden III

Edward J. McFadden III has three published novels *The Black Death of Babylon*, *Our Dying Land*, and *Hoaxers*. His short fiction has appeared in numerous magazines and anthologies. For more information about Ed, go to edwardmcfadden.com.

Rain fell in torrents, limiting Jerry's visibility. The windshield of his Corvette was a blur of water, and the cars in front of him were stopping, some pulling to the side of the road, others reducing their speed to a crawl. Jerry rotated his head slowly, cracking his neck as he tried in vain to remain patient. The rain eased a bit, and Jerry jerked on the wheel, pulling onto the road's thin shoulder. He stomped the gas pedal, sending grass and gravel flying, and eliciting a series of honks and single finger salutes as he sped around the snarled traffic.

As he increased speed, he saw the train tracks ahead, the gentle rise of the road, and Jerry braked. The black Corvette hydroplaned, and then came back into alignment. Red lights shined as warning gates lowered across the road, stopping traffic for an oncoming train. Jerry thought he could beat the gates, and pressed the gas pedal to the floor, and the Corvette lurched forward, engine screaming. But it wasn't even close. Jerry stomped on the brake, and the 'vette skidded, the white gate with red flashing lights slashing down across the road.

"Shit!" shrieked Jerry, as he slammed the steering wheel and waited for the train to pass. He was headed home, and there was really no rush, but his frustration was boiling over nonetheless.

A white cross on a utility pole caught his attention just as the rain picked up again in earnest, pounding the car's roof so hard individual drops couldn't be distinguished. A makeshift shrine had been constructed around a pole next to the tracks, its large white cross clearly visible through the crushing rain.

Jerry felt strange. The rain chose that moment to back off, and Jerry saw a thin ray of sunlight peeking through the thick clouds.

On the ground before the utility pole there was a blue box with glass windows and a candle inside, and all around it were candles of various colors and sizes, all having burned to nothing but stubs and blackened wicks. A teddy bear with a red ribbon held court over the scene, which also included several shells, a small plastic sheriffs' badge, and a dead plant in a gray plastic container. "I Love You" was painted in white lettering on a piece of wood propped against the pole, but the name below the message was no longer legible.

As Jerry's eyes moved up the utility pole, he saw that the white cross was just below a brass plaque that showed the pole's number, 496, in black lettering over brass. Around the cross were a series of fake flowers, and handwritten notes, most of which had been destroyed by the weather, but as Jerry squinted to read one of the notes, his eyes widened.

A cracked plastic picture holder had been nailed to the pole just below the cross, and in it were photos of *him*. In the center, his high school picture stared back at him, his own eyes mocking him through the rain.

He reeled, his head slamming into the seat's headrest. He rubbed his eyes, and struggled to see through the rain, but the pictures were clearly of him. In addition to his high school photo, there was a picture of him in his little league uniform, him standing in his tuxedo the night of his prom, and another with him wearing his black graduation robes.

His mind swam, and he heard the train whistle blaring through the rain. He paid it no mind as he exited his car, and headed for the shrine. He was drenched by the time he reached the telephone pole, but he just stood there, gawking at his pictures. Broken shells and a carefully constructed ring of stones circled his memorial, and now Jerry saw some coins, a plastic ring, and a statue of a black and white dog that resembled Frodo, a springer spaniel from his youth.

The rain picked-up, and Jerry wiped his face, transfixed, and so it was that he didn't see the young boy approach until he was right next to him.

"Mister?" questioned the boy, and Jerry jumped.

The boy had blue eyes, short dirty blonde hair, and a face full of red freckles. He looked familiar, but Jerry couldn't place the child. The boy stood in the pouring rain, but didn't appear to be wet at all.

"Mister?" the boy said again, looking up at Jerry with lost eyes. "I'm gettin' out of the rain."

Jerry took a hesitant step, and then looked down the train tracks in both directions; nothing but trees, the railroad tracks, and an ordered line of utility poles. The boy began walking along the tracks, singing to himself, and ignoring Jerry.

"Wait," he yelled, but the boy didn't stop. Instead, he turned and headed into the woods. Jerry lurched forward, passing the next pole, which was numbered 495. At first he couldn't see where the boy had entered the forest, but as he continued down the railroad tracks, the entrance to a path became visible. The boy stood there, just inside the forest, beckoning for him to follow, and Jerry did.

"Why were you looking at the shrine?" asked Jerry of the boy. "Did you know the person who died?" Then the image of his pictures behind the cracked plastic came rushing back, and he swayed on his feet, bracing himself against a tree.

The rain eased to a drizzle beneath the thick canopy of trees, and the boy waited, watching Jerry with his hard blue eyes. "You want to tell me what…" Jerry's voice trailed off when he saw the dead animals hanging from a large oak tree behind the boy.

Dead frogs hung from the tree's branches next to a dog, a cat, and several corpses that were so rotted and decayed Jerry could no longer tell what they had been. The smell of rot, mixed with the fresh scent of rain, assailed Jerry's senses, and he gagged and threw up in his mouth. Small headstones and rocks painted with pet names surrounded the tree.

Large rusted fishhooks impaled each frog through the head, most through an eye cavity. There were six of them, and several still had blood dripping from them, and globular eyes hanging from their sockets. The cat hung from its tail, and had been there for some time, its fur hanging on nothing but bones, its eyes gone. As Jerry made his way through the makeshift cemetery toward the tree, the dog's head lolled to one side, its empty eye sockets tracking him.

The corpses swung gently in the breeze, and Jerry covered his nose, but the smell just got stronger. The tree canopy was getting wetter, and more rain was making its way through. Something landed on his foot and he jumped. A frog sat on the ground before him, its glassy eyes staring up at him as if asking a question.

With a suddenness that knocked Jerry from his feet, the frog exploded, splattering him with blood, skin, and entrails.

The boy stood over him. "What? I thought you would like that," said the boy. When Jerry didn't answer, the boy asked, "I thought you liked blowing up frogs?"

Jerry's face twisted, and he got to his feet. He and Tommy had blown up frogs when they were kids by putting M80's inside the frog's mouth, or trapping it in a bucket and tossing the explosive in. Oh, how they would laugh, and tell their friends.

The boy was next to Jerry, staring up at him. Jerry's hand shot out and grabbed the boy by the wrist. "Where the hell did you get the fireworks? And why would you do that? Who taught you to do that?" screamed Jerry.

"Why, you of course," answered the boy, his cold blue eyes never leaving Jerry's.

"Well, we'll see what your mother thinks," said Jerry, as he pulled the boy through the small graveyard back up the path toward the railroad tracks.

A black and white dog blocked the pathway, and the boy giggled. When Jerry tried to get past the animal, it growled, and then barked. "What the hell is your problem?"

"Don't remember him, huh?" said the boy.

Jerry screamed, tried to speak, and then fell like an oak after it's been sawed. Sticks began protruding from the dog as it barked, white foam dripping from its mouth. Broken broom handles, metal rebar, and the twisted shaft of a golf club rose from the dog's flesh. The animal yelped and growled, and Jerry got to his feet, and backed down the path the way he had come.

When he turned to run, an old red brick building that looked like an old castle stood in his way, where only moments before forest had stretched as far as he could see.

"You were so happy when they tore it down. Weren't you?" The boy was there again, his big blue eyes and hard stare unnerving.

"How do you know about that?" snapped Jerry, his face dark, eyes blazing.

The boy stepped forward, took Jerry's hand, and led him into the structure.

The old textile mill had been demolished back in 1995, but it had served as the primary location for many deeds of debauchery for Jerry and his friends throughout their youth. The building Jerry remembered was made of crumbling red brick and rusted metal, and the interior was like the surface of another planet—rusted metal dust on the floor like sand, and huge rusted machines all around, barely discernible as their former shapes, dotting the landscape like tiny rusted mountains.

In one corner, two boys poked a dog with sticks, laughing and hooting as they did so. Jerry took a step forward, and then stopped as recognition washed over him. His childhood friend Peter was unmistakable. Jerry smiled, remembering his friend who had died of prostate cancer several years prior. Peter and a young version of himself thrust their sticks forward, impaling the dog as it yelped and growled, then finally lay still.

Both boys dropped their sticks in unison, as if they didn't fully realize what they had been doing. Then young Jerry started to run. "Wait," yelled Peter, as he took up chase.

Peter was much faster and young Jerry didn't even make it out of the building before Peter tackled him, and both boys landed hard on brown steel dust. "You can't tell anyone! You hear me? We didn't mean it and we can say a prayer in church this week and we'll be forgiven," yelled Peter.

Young Jerry stopped struggling and nodded, and old Jerry fell to his knees, closing his eyes, his head falling into his hands. "The dog's name was

Ralph. Did you know that?" asked the boy.

Rain drops splattered off Jerry's jacket, and ran down his face. The sharp *puff* of a BB gun firing made Jerry's head jerk upright. The red brick building was gone, replaced by wet forest. Young Jerry and Peter ran through the woods, shooting as they went. Peter stopped right in front of old Jerry, knelt, shouldered his rifle, and fired. Then he was up and running, pumping the gun as he went.

A shriek that sounded like a baby wailing in pain filled Jerry's mind. He ran down the path toward the sound, and arrived in a clearing just in time to watch his younger self pump a BB into the head of the cat he had seen hanging from the cemetery tree. Peter rushed up and put another piece of copper into the animal, yelling and hooting as young Jerry looked at the dead animal with glazed eyes.

Jerry had seen enough. Curiosity had drawn him after the boy, and into the woods, but his wife was waiting for him at home with a chilled martini and a warm fire. He turned and headed back down the path.

The boy took Jerry's hand, pulling him back into the woods. Jerry fought to free himself, but the boy's grip was vise-like. "I know you loved animals. But you love people more," said the boy. As Jerry tugged his arm, trying to free himself, rows of desks filled the woods, each with a mannequin sitting at it.

Except for one.

A thin black-haired boy, with lanky arms and legs sat at one of the desks, his head bowed. The sound of the rain faded, replaced by taunting and heckling. "Your Dad was gay. That's why he died. Are you gay, Vic? Or do you go by Vicky now? Do you like boys like your dead dad did?"

Tears streamed down Vic's face, and he reached into his jacket, and drew out a pocket knife. As he opened it, he looked around at the mannequins as they sat at their desks, then he plunged the knife into his chest and screamed, blood spurting across the desk, and spattering on a tree. The boy fell forward, falling through the desk as he and everything around him turned to dust, and was blown away on the wind.

The sound of rain hitting the tree canopy roared in Jerry's ears as he stood transfixed, staring at the spot where young Vic had been.

"He was a friend of yours, no?" Jerry nodded. "And you did nothing?" Jerry nodded again. "A familiar theme with you," said the boy, and Jerry felt a tingle run though him, and he had a surge of recognition, and looked at the boy. Then the thought was gone.

"He lived at least," said Jerry.

"Yeah," said the boy. "You'd think that his father killing himself because another police officer outed him as gay, and to get tormented about it by just about everybody he came in contact with, should have been enough shame to crush his life. But it didn't. What's your excuse?"

"You know I..." Jerry looked for the boy, but he was gone. Rain fell, and thunder cracked in the distance, and all the trees seemed to have eyes, their branches swaying and clutching at Jerry as he made his way down the path toward the railroad tracks.

Jerry started to run when he saw the window of rain at the end of the forest. He smirked and looked over his shoulder, the little boy nowhere to be seen. He burst from the trees, the echo of the train whistle getting louder, and he found himself standing at the end of an alleyway. The night was deep, rain gone, but dark clouds obscured the sky. An old vagrant hobbled by him on the cracked sidewalk, and looked his way. Maggots swam in the man's eyes, and he chuckled, turning away and heading across the street toward an old burnt-out house.

Jerry remembered the scene, and looked up the street in panic. A blue Mustang raced over the hill, its fog lights cutting through the night. The old man turned, and looked at Jerry again, and the Mustang skidded in an attempt to avoid the vagrant, but failed. The old man was tossed up the street twenty feet by the impact, and landed hard. The pile of gray rags didn't move, and Jerry gasped. The Mustang came to a halt, paused for a minute, and then took off up the road into the night.

"You swore you'd never tell anyone, right? Just like Peter and the dog. But you did tell, Jerry. Didn't you?" The boy was back, and Jerry jumped at the sound of his voice.

"There's no way you could know this. It was an accident," said Jerry, almost pleading.

"You seem to have a lot of them," said the boy. "You still don't remember me? There's still time. I can still help you in time."

Jerry racked his brain, but the boy looked like many ten-year-olds: blue eyes, ruffled blond hair, freckles. Then it hit him, and the fact that it had taken him so long sent bile creeping up his throat. He had only seen the boy once, and not for long, but Jerry couldn't help but think he had blocked the memory.

"Toby?" asked Jerry, and the boy smiled. The day Jerry had first seen Toby was the day Toby's dad had murdered his only son.

Jerry had been walking Neo, his black lab, and hid behind an evergreen when Dr. Jennings came tear-assing around the corner and skidded to a stop in a driveway marked with a sign that read: Jennings 586. The door to his BMW flew open, and the doctor got out carrying a handgun and an axe. As he approached his front door, Jerry slinked across the street, staying out of sight, and when Jennings kicked in his front door, Jerry went to the side of the house and watched through a window as the doctor killed his cheating wife.

Toby had been in his room, playing with his new train set he had gotten for his birthday. The locomotive's whistle blew, and smoke poured from the engine's stack as the train went around in a figure eight. There was a railroad crossing on one end, and three matchbox cars sat on a road made of black construction paper, one of which was a black Corvette.

Jennings burst through the boy's door and Toby turned, looking out the window at Jerry. Jennings screamed at the boy in a drunken rage, and then cleaved him with the axe. Jerry fell backward into a rose bush as blood spattered the window. Neo started barking, and a gunshot rocked the night as Dr. Jennings took the easy way out.

Jerry hurried away back toward his house. Why should he get involved? They were all dead and there was no way he could change that. He'd have to tell everything, explain why he didn't do anything. Toby's train went around and around on its track, and the last thing Jerry saw before he heard the loud blaring of the train whistle, was the black Corvette matchbox car getting smashed to pieces by the toy train.

The boy stared with large blue eyes that were calling for Jerry to follow him into that thin ray of sunlight.

And follow Jerry did.

ATHEISTS IN THE CEMETERY
Meredith Morgenstern

Meredith Morgenstern writes historical fantasy, dark paranormal, and Twilight Zone-esque speculative fiction. Her YA short story, *The Esther* is included in Spencer Hill Press's 2013 anthology, *Holiday Magic*. She lives in Brooklyn, New York, with her husband and two children. They can see Green-Wood Cemetery from their living room window.

Even Jude behaves himself on trips to Green-Wood Cemetery. It's almost as if the respectful peace and quiet seeps into his two-year-old brain and gives him some sort of signal that he should not cry or screech or run there. We still bring the stroller – Green-Wood is extremely hilly, with steep slopes that leave even healthy grown-ups breathless. The trees and grass, the breezes blowing in from New York Harbor less than a mile away, add an almost bucolic quality to the air. We city dwellers will take that wherever we can get it. At times we let Jude out of the stroller so he can stretch his little legs. The wind blows his fine blond hair into tufts like a baby chick. He walks and looks around, stopping occasionally to pat a gravestone with his dimpled hand or tickle the toes of a marble angel.

Jacob, now five, practices his new reading skills on the grave markers. I walk beside him and mindlessly run my fingers through his thick black hair, inherited from his Hispanic father. Now and then I have to help him work his way around some of the more complicated family names, foreign names from way back with too many vowels or too many consonants. Names shortened by living descendants in the past generation or two. That's just how it works in America: Grabowsky becomes Grabo, Rosenblatt becomes Rosen, Monteluciano becomes Monte. The dead don't mind; they're in the past where they belong.

The cemetery itself is enormous, even by urban standards. In a city where real estate is a prime commodity more sought after than gold, Green-Wood takes up nearly five-hundred acres. Over half a million people are buried under the soft green grass, in the sides of the steep hills, near the lakes, or under the gnarled old trees. In the autumn, the cemetery bursts with color like any other park, in hues of red, orange and yellow. From the crest of Battle Hill, the highest point in Brooklyn, you can see New York Harbor, downtown Brooklyn, and on clear days, even the Manhattan skyline.

On this particular day in late September it's still warm enough that the leaves have not yet begun to turn, and the kids only need hoodies. No winter coats yet, no hats or gloves. In the shade, when the wind blows, a hint of the chill to come might sting a bit. Otherwise it's sunny and warm-ish, and those of us old enough to know what's coming soak it in and store it away for the long winter months ahead.

We stop by one of the lakes to rest before we make the push up Battle Hill. Jude chases some geese along the grassy slope. Luis chases Jude to make sure he doesn't fall into the stagnant, brown water. I plop down in the shade of a cherry blossom tree and take out my water bottle. Leaning toward Jacob, I run my finger under the letters of my own name on the plastic: "Alicia Perez." Next to me, Jacob's already not paying attention, the reading lessons over for the day. He systematically inserts pretzel sticks into his mouth. Across the lake, a neighbor of ours sits with his daughter. They throw bread crusts to the geese. We wave. I stare at the water and let my thoughts wander.

"What's that?" Jacob interrupts my daze.

I follow his finger to a small rectangular granite stone placed flat in the ground. A rosary sits on top of the stone. It's too perfectly arranged to have been dropped randomly. Someone placed it there, and recently.

"That's someone's grave." I know that's not what he meant, but I'm a Jewish mother raising my child without religion and don't feel like explaining rosaries right this second.

He's too smart and won't let me get away with it. "I know, Mom." Sometimes the teenager he'll be in a few years comes out in the put-upon tones of voice he adopts when he knows I'm being either patronizing or condescending. "I know that's a stone for a dead person. But what's that on it? It looks like a necklace."

In my head I sigh an *Oy vey*. Why can't he ask his father? Luis is the most lapsed Catholic anyone could possibly be.

In our neighborhood we're considered the norm, good liberal parents like everyone else, raising our kids right: organic foods, pro-everything progressive. With self-satisfied smugness we swap stories with our peers of raising this generation to know the consequences of their own actions and not fear petty punishment from some supposedly divine, but ultimately capricious, being that probably doesn't even exist. In our part of Brooklyn, atheism is a point of pride.

"It's called a rosary, sweetheart." I don't like having these conversations with Jacob. He's too bright, too inquisitive, too bold. All good qualities, except when he pounces on a subject I don't want to talk about, like God.

"Is it a necklace?"

"Some people wear it as one, sure. Remember the time Grandma Vivian took you to church? Remember that?"

"Yes."

"Well, Grandma Vivian is called a Catholic. That's one of the types of people who believe in God. And Catholics like rosaries. They count the beads and pray with each bead as they count."

He thinks about this for a while. I offer him my hand. "Want to walk over and see it?"

It takes me several seconds to make sense of the math from the dates on the gravestone. My mind simply refuses to acknowledge the reality. Green-Wood is full of dead babies and children, so this shouldn't surprise or horrify me. Yet, there it is, chiseled into granite.

August 24, 1973 – August 26, 1973.

Jacob knows his numbers and can do simple arithmetic, but the four digit years throw him off. When he asks, I don't lie. After I tell him how old the person in the grave below us was at the time of her death he's quiet. I check his face. Thankfully he seems more thoughtful than upset.

"Why did someone put a rosary here?"

"I don't know. It's a thing some people do, I guess. A show of love and respect for the dead."

In that way kids his age have of being utterly blunt while missing the point, he says, "But the baby in that grave can't pray. Two-day olds don't know how to pray, and also she's dead."

"Right." My thoughts move quickly. I have to explain this at his level. "This little girl had a mommy and maybe a daddy, too. People loved her and miss her, even after all these years. To show that love, someone left this rosary so that the rest of us can see. Here," I squat down and pick up a jagged white stone. "I'm Jewish, which means you're Jewish. Do you know what Jewish people do at graves?"

He shakes his head, still staring at the baby's marker. His coarse black hair doesn't move in the wind the way Jude's hair does.

"We leave stones for the dead. We put them there as a way of saying hello to the dead person, to let them know someone is still thinking of them." I place the stone next to the rosary. My knees creak and pop as I stand back up.

"But, Mommy." Ah, now that he's confused and thoughtful I'm back to being "Mommy." "You and Daddy told me that dead people are just dead. They don't see or feel or hear anything. They don't think anything. So how do they know if we leave them a stone?"

I take a deep breath and remind myself that this is better than having a stupid child, one without critical thinking skills.

"It's just a thing Jewish people do." I snap it out harsher than I intended. While I want him to keep asking questions, I don't necessarily want to have to keep answering them. It's hard to explain being Jewish without references to God. He's still too young to understand the nuances between Judaism the religion, which I gave up long ago, and being Jewish as an ethnicity, which is as much a part of our family heritage and culture as being Cuban is for Luis.

Jacob takes it in stride. "I want to leave a stone for someone." He scans the ground.

"For who?"

"I don't know yet. Help me find a perfect stone."

"What's a perfect stone?"

"I don't know yet."

With those crystal clear instructions I search for stones of varying size, texture and color. None of them meet Jacob's ineffable standards.

The wind picks up, and Luis brings Jude back to our side of the lake. Now that the little one has had a chance to walk around a bit he doesn't protest when we strap him in to the stroller for the long, sharp climb to the top of Battle Hill. Luis digs a sippy cup out of the diaper bag and Jude sucks down some water.

Jacob huffs and puffs, taking the hill in exaggerated steps that make the most of his long legs. He never takes his eyes off the ground, searching for that perfect stone intended for an unknown dead person.

I mentally pat myself on the back for my parenting skills. This is one reason why we do bring the kids here: to teach them respect for death and the dead. It's not an easy concept to grasp without defaulting to some sort of afterlife. Bringing them here helps get across the point of death's finality and peacefulness.

The top of Battle Hill is crowded with tourists and families like us, looking for a slice of quiet in the big bad city. An old couple sits on the bench near the statue of Minerva, who raises a hand in salute to her statue sister Liberty out in New York Harbor. Luis takes Jacob to see the bronze soldiers at the Civil War memorial. I push Jude around, the placards detailing the Battle of Brooklyn that took place here during the Revolution and gave the hill its name.

Jacob runs back to me. Luis and I let him; up here there are more memorials and statues than graves, so we don't consider running to be disrespectful. No one around us seems to mind. No one comes to Battle Hill to mourn, even if it is in the middle of a graveyard.

"Did you get a stone?"

"No." He spreads his hands, empty. "The trees over there look like they have eyes."

"Do they?"

"Yeah, look."

I've seen the trees many times but I indulge him and look. I'm too much of an urban princess to know what types of trees they are. They're gnarled, bloated and ugly, the trunks a light grey with natural swirls that look like eyes.

"Maybe the trees are watching us." Jacob goes back to searching the ground for a perfect stone, missing my smile and wink.

"Trees don't really have eyes, Mom."

"I know, sweetheart." I ruffle his hair. He ducks away from me. "I was making a joke."

"It's not nice to make jokes in a cemetery. People like peace and quiet and fresh air here." He takes a dramatically deep breath to emphasize his point.

Duly chastised, I let Luis take over stroller duty and lead the way down the hill.

"Maybe," Jacob muses, "The people buried here put their eyes into the tree so they can watch us."

He's so matter-of-fact about this that it sends a shiver across the back of my neck. I remind myself that being five years old doesn't give him any special insight into death. Children are not preternatural, just imaginative.

Without warning, Jacob runs past me. We're at the long curve on the side of the hill and can't see cars coming toward us. I call after him. He ignores me and scrambles up a vertical slab of dirt beneath a row of graves. Only when he's fully off the road, and no cars come screeching around the bend, do I exhale.

"I found it!"

When I catch up to him I'm clutching my chest as much in a terror hangover as from breathlessness.

"Jacob! Do not run past me like that, especially on these big curves. If a car came around-."

"I found my stone." He already knows how to tune out my lecture voice.

In the amber light and darkening shadows, I see a softly rounded stone that fits perfectly into Jacob's small palm. He holds it like a prize.

Luis comes chasing after us, knuckles white from anxiety and from holding the stroller against gravity pulling it down the hillside and off the drop behind one of the cemetery's public lots.

"Jacob! Don't you ever-."

I shake my head at him. Jacob won't hear us now. Later, when all is calm and we can ensure we have Jacob's full attention, we'll revisit the matter. What's important is that he didn't get hurt and we need to move on.

"Now I need to find someone to give it to." Jacob looks around, as if the right grave will jump up and present itself.

"Come on." Luis reaches up to help Jacob down from the raised plot. "I'm sure we'll see someone you can give that to on our way out."

One of the borders of the cemetery is Brooklyn's Fifth Avenue. On the other side of Fifth Ave is a bakery. The wind changes direction and we all catch a whiff of fresh-baked bread.

My stomach rumbles. "I wonder if the dead get hungry when they smell that."

"I told you, Mom. The dead can't smell anything because they're dead. Remember?"

"Maybe they're jealous they can't eat anymore."

Jacob growls, his way of warning us he's not in the mood to joke. Luis and I share a look, laughing silently behind our child's back.

We take Perimeter Road to the exit, which runs alongside Fifth Ave. Here it's quieter than the rest of the cemetery, the smell of bread stronger. There aren't any famous people buried in this area, or gaudy mausoleums to gawk at, or beautiful angel statues reaching toward the sky or weeping over the departed. No monuments or memorials to attract tourists. Just very old gravestones so weather-beaten we can hardly read the names. Here, the trees – the trees with eyes – have taken over the landscape, their roots pushing up through the road, their low-hanging branches in my face and pulling my hair. The shadows thicken here, in the part of the cemetery where trees outnumber visitors. The back of my neck prickles again. My better sense takes a break and my imagination runs wild for a moment. I fall back and put my hand over Luis's on the stroller's handle.

Jacob clutches his stone tight in his fist. After a while, at some signal only he can hear or see, he veers off the road and into the burial lot. We watch him until he stops at one of the graves. I let go of Luis and chase after him.

"Who is this?" he asks.

I read the name and dates in silence first and have to pull myself together to read them out loud, not only because of the difficulty of the last name, but because of the coincidence of the dates. "This was a little boy. His name was Elias Roschenkrantzky and he lived in the 1880s. He was five years old when he died. Actually," I take a deep breath and brace myself. "His birthday was the same as yours, October 8th. But he was born more than a hundred years before you."

His eyes open wide. With as much reverence as he can muster at his age, Jacob dusts some dirt off the top of Elias Roschenkrantzky's grave marker. He places his stone there and lets his fingers linger. The branches and leaves of the trees around us rustle and stir, creating shadows on the trunks that come and go in the fading light. The trees look like they're blinking. I tell myself it's getting chilly and that's why I'm suddenly anxious to leave.

On the way home we pick up some San Francisco-style sourdough bread, fresh out of the bakery ovens. For dinner we break it apart and eat it with cheese, butter, and slices of salami. After Jude goes to bed, Luis and I sit on the couch with Jacob for that overdue talk about running off. He listens patiently, nods and agrees in all the right places. When we're done, he picks up where we left off at the cemetery.

He wants to know about Elias Roschenkrantzky, and why Jews leave stones, and what happens to the stones, and next time we go can he bring a toy to leave for Elias Roschenkrantzky?

"Elias is dead, sweetheart." I stroke his hair and kiss his cheek. His face retains a hint of the delicious baby fat that has been melting away too quickly for me. The angles of his cheekbones and jawline are still soft, the skin still smooth. But the round chubbiness is gone. Because we got home so late I let the kids skip their baths tonight. Jacob smells so perfect I want to bite into his cheek. He smells like baby and earth, like trees and wind, like bread and life.

"But, Mom." I pull back before he can push my face away. "If we leave stones, why can't we leave toys?"

"Dead people can't play with toys," Luis answers. "That's very sweet of you, though."

When Jacob goes to bed I get the insane idea to look Elias Roschenkrantzky up on the Internet. I tell myself it's so I'll be prepared when Jacob inevitably asks more questions about him. Somewhere deep inside me, though, comes the insistent feeling that I'm doing this to prove to myself that Jacob is not Elias, that they don't have too much in common. Maybe I can protect Jacob from death forever by breaking the cycle of coincidences beyond their ages, birthdays, and Jewishness.

I stay up well past my usual bedtime scouring the web for some archived family photo of this dead kid. There are plenty of blogs keeping track of people's search for ancestors. Americans love to learn about where they come from, especially when they are several generations removed from those who immigrated here. Each wave of immigrants has an army of record-keepers who post photos, letters, and passenger tickets for all posterity to admire. I even check the Ellis Island passenger records. There are ship manifests containing family names similar to Roschenkrantzky. No first names of Elias in the records. Maybe he was born here in America. I try looking up birth records from the 1880s, expanding my search from Brooklyn to all five boroughs of New York, and even New Jersey, Boston and Philadelphia. Nothing comes up. This shouldn't surprise or upset me; records from the time weren't great, especially for poor immigrant families. Yet, I feel defeated.

When I finally go to bed I fall asleep still thinking about Elias. I wake up with a macabre shadow over me from dreaming about dead little boys.

123

The following weekend is the first in October, days before Jacob – and Elias's – birthday. Jacob wants to see if his stone is still on Elias's tomb. With no other plans and the weather as perfect as New York is capable of getting, we take a lazy stroll back to Green-Wood cemetery.

This time when we pass the entrance we make a sharp right for Perimeter Road instead of heading straight toward Battle Hill. I let Luis take Jude to the lake while I help Jacob find Elias's tomb.

The grave marker is there, next to a tree with eyes that glow and stare in the bright midday sunlight.

"Where's the stone?"

My heartbeat quickens and I come to the realization I'm holding my breath. I shove my hands into my hoodie pockets to hide their trembling.

"I don't know, sweetheart. Maybe someone knocked it off by accident."

Jacob leans over the top of the tombstone and sounds out the words, words written in squiggly handwriting like a child's, scratched onto the grey granite as if written with a rock.

THANK YOU JACOB

"Mommy?" Jacob takes my hand. I'm not sure he's aware he's doing it. I squeeze his hand and pull him close. "Who wrote that? Why does it say my name?"

"Um…someone…uh…" I detest these moments of being caught so off-guard, with no ready answer.

"I think it was Elias." He looks at me to confirm or deny his hypothesis, eyes wide and the corners of his mouth turned down.

I put my arm around his shoulder and guide him away, back toward the road. He has to jog to keep up. "I think it was Elias," he says again, between huffs of breath. "I think he saw the stone we left. Sometimes you could be wrong, you know, Mom."

I can't think of anything to reply.

FAMILY BUSINESS
g. Elmer Munson

g. Elmer Munson is a New England writer of all things strange and unusual as well as the horrors of everyday life. He has published numerous short stories as well as the novel *Stripped*, the story collection *Tales From The Underground*, and the upcoming novella *Camp Hollybrook*. He has more works in progress than can be counted, so you can follow his (mis)adventures on the web at gElmerMunson.com.

Johan answered the door and stepped back. His mouth hung open and his eyes grew wide. For just a moment he ignored the screaming wind and stared at the vaguely familiar beauty before him. As the rain poured down behind her, she whipped her golden hair around, spraying him ever so slightly. He didn't mind; actually, he barely noticed.

"Johan," his mother called from the hall. "Close the door, you'll let the storm in." He listened as her soft slippers padded on the hardwood floor and stopped when she entered the kitchen. "Who are you?" she asked. "Johan, who is this?"

Johan opened his mouth but no words would come. He couldn't take his eyes off the young woman in the doorway.

She smiled at Johan before leaning to the side to look at his mother. "I beg your pardon, ma'am," she said. "I've been lost in the rain, and your castle is the first thing I've seen. I wonder if I could trouble you for some warmth and perhaps a chance to dry off."

Johan's mother stared at her for a moment before shifting her eyes to the frenzied storm beyond. "Well, close the door," she said as she waved her in the house. "Johan, fetch her some towels. She must be freezing."

Johan cleared his throat. "Of course," he said. "At once." He stepped back and shuffled towards the hall without pulling his eyes away. The young woman let out a soft laugh when Johan nearly tripped over a chair.

"Johan."

"Sorry, Mother," he said as he spun on his heel and ran out of the room. He took the stairs two at a time and grabbed a towel from the linen closet.

He nearly fell on the way back down and burst into the kitchen just as his mother was pulling a chair towards the stove. She glanced at him with a frown before turning to their guest.

"Have a seat by the fire." His mother reached her hand out for the towel, and Johan shuffled forward with his head down to hand it over. "What brings you out on a night like this?"

"I got lost."

"So you said. What's your name?"

"Gwen."

"Of course, Gwen." Johan said. "*Professor* Gwen?"

She blushed and looked at the floor. "Please," she said in a small voice. "Just call me Gwen."

"A bit young to be a professor," Johan's mother said with one raised eyebrow. "And how do you know each other?"

Johan knew that look and before she could say more he stepped forward. "Professor Gwen teaches archeology at the university," he said. "I met her during last season's fair."

"You? Spoke to a professor?" his mother asked.

"Well," Johan began before looking down at the floor.

"I spoke to him," Gwen said.

Johan's mother shot her a look. "Well, you won't get very far with this one," she said.

"*Mother!*"

"Well, she won't," Johan's mother said. "*You'll* never go to university. You can barely tie your shoes." Johan looked down at the floor and said nothing. His mother stared at Gwen as she dried her hair by the fire. They all shared an uncomfortable silence and might have remained that way if the door hadn't blown open. "Great goodness," his mother screamed as the wind blew chunks of hail across the kitchen. "Johan, get it closed."

Johan threw himself against the door and slammed the bar into place. His feet slipped in the puddle and spread in opposite directions. He had to cling to the bar to keep from falling. Behind him, Gwen giggled and his mother let out a displeased "Hrrmph."

"Well, we can't have you going out in this weather," his mother said. "You'll have to stay with us."

"Thank you kindly," Gwen said. "I'm not certain I could find my way back to the village at this point."

"Don't you worry, dear. Johan will fix things up for you." She turned towards the door and barked "Johan," over her shoulder as she headed out of the kitchen. She marched down the hall, hung a left past the guest room, and headed down the back stairs.

"Mother?" Johan asked. He slowed and pointed towards the guest room door, but his mother did not stop.

"She's not staying there," she said. "She's staying down here."

"But –that's storage," Johan said. "Where will she sleep?"

"There's a mattress." She reached the bottom of the stairs and continued down the short hall.

"Yes, but it's not exactly comfortable."

"So what?" She reached the last door and stopped to turn around. She glanced past Johan before dropping her voice. "I don't want that girl snooping around."

"But mother–"

"No buts," she interrupted. "I don't know her and I don't like her. She can stay down here. And don't you get any ideas about visiting her in the middle of the night either, because I'll be listening."

Johan blushed and looked at the floor but said nothing.

His mother cracked open the storage room door and looked inside.

Johan instinctively took a step back. "What about Father?" he asked.

His mother twirled around and grabbed him by the shoulder, slamming him against the wall.

"You shut your goddamn mouth," she said, her face so close to his he could smell the whiskey she'd been drinking. "That's family business." He could hear the plaster wall behind him begin to crack. With a final push, she let go, brushed dust from his shoulder, and straightened his collar. She stepped back and smiled. "Never mind about that, let's just get your little friend set up for the night."

"Yes, Mother."

***

Gwen followed Johan down the stairs. She didn't remember him from the fair but that didn't surprise her. She'd met hundreds of people that day and wouldn't recognize most of them if they walked up and bit her. She spent so much of her time at the university that everyone else tended to look the same.

Johan, however, seemed different. He didn't talk much, but he looked like he was always thinking about something. So many people surrounded her with talk, spending every bit of their energy trying to impress her. It was refreshing to spend a little time with someone else in silence. Maybe if she asked, he would even listen to her. That was something no one else did.

He reached the bottom of the stairs, turned left, and slowed. There was a door at the far end of the hall but not much else. There were no windows or photos on the walls. There were no other doors. He hesitated but headed towards it without saying a word.

"Johan?" She asked. He remained silent as he crept the final few steps to the door. "Johan?"

"What?" He flinched and spun around, his eyes wide and his face losing some of its color.

"Are you okay?"

"Yeah, fine," he said. He cleared his throat and reached for the handle. "Never better. Just...thinking." He opened the door and stepped to the side, allowing Gwen to enter what would be her lodging for the night.

It was an odd little room, mostly empty except for a line of boxes to one side. The only furnishing was a single mattress against the far wall. There was no frame or box spring, but the bed was made up with cotton sheets and a single pillow. A wooden crate with a candleholder resting on top sat at one end like a makeshift headboard. It wasn't the most inviting bed in the world, but at least she was out of the rain.

"Well, this looks cozy," she said.

"Sorry," he said without looking at her. "It was Mother's idea. She said you'd be more comfortable down here."

"Oh. Okay." She moved in closer and touched the mattress. It didn't *feel* very comfortable, and the sheets were very thin. She was still chilly from the rain. "Any chance of getting a blanket?" she asked. She turned around in time to see the door closing. With a click she was alone. "Okay then," she whispered. "I'll take that as a no."

She walked around the room and peeked in a few of the boxes. They held nothing more than binders full of paperwork. No blankets. She checked the wooden crate but it looked to be nailed shut. *Brilliant*, she thought. She stripped off her still damp clothes and put on the robe that Johan's mother had given her. It was far too big, but at least it was dry.

Gwen gave one last look around the room but there was nothing to see. There were no windows, but considering the storm raging outside she didn't mind very much. The walls were nothing more than stacked rock and mortar, clearly the castle's foundation. The floor was bare concrete. She laid down on the bed, dropped her head on the pillow, and closed her eyes.

The silence of the room was almost magical, but something wasn't right. She couldn't hear anything, but she felt the room move. It was barely noticeable, but with the mattress directly on the floor she could feel everything shake ever so slightly. She rolled to her side, but the mattress was so small, she fell off.

She climbed back on the bed, curled up in a little ball, and tried to ignore it. It didn't work. *Great*, she thought as she sat up. She laid her hand on the floor. The vibration seemed to be coming from under the concrete floor. She felt around and found that it was strongest right under the wooden crate.

Gwen pushed against the crate but it only moved slightly. It scraped against the floor so loud she stopped and held her breath. There was no noise from the hall. She felt around the crate but found no easy way to open it up. It was nailed shut and she didn't have a hammer.

She went back to the boxes and started to search. She moved binders to the side and checked underneath. After three boxes she was about ready to give up, but the fourth box had a leather case. Inside she found a bizarre collection of tools the likes of which she had only seen drawings. Some were obviously meant for digging, while others had no discernible purpose.

With the case was an oddly-bound binder. Gwen flipped it open and scanned the contents. Although the language was foreign to her, she recognized some of the symbols. She had seen similar images as a graduate student in Egypt. Some of her old anthropology texts had similar writings, but she'd never seen them in their original form.

The crate behind her thumped and she spun around. The floor vibrated and the wood shifted. She reached in the leather case and pulled out the closest thing to a hammer she could find. It was a curved trowel with a solid metal handle. She slid the tip under the crate and kicked it in. The crate shifted back and rose up enough for her to take a look.

Underneath the crate laid a rough cut trap door, a brass ring bolted to the center. The opening wasn't very big, but looked just wide enough to fit a small adult. *What the hell?* She looked over her shoulder but the room door stood closed tight. No sound came from the hall. She looked back at the stacks of paperwork and the bizarre images contained inside.

She brought her legs up and shoved the crate as hard as she could. *What am I thinking?* She wondered, before the door came into full view. *I guess one peek can't hurt.*

Gwen grabbed the brass ring and pulled. A rough stone staircase descended into the darkness below. A breeze blew across her face with a smell that was unpleasant yet somehow familiar. She grabbed the leather case, the binder, and the room's only candleholder. Without hesitation, she headed down.

***

Johan sat at the breakfast table with his mother. The storm outside was ferocious, even worse than the previous night, but they behaved as if it wasn't even there. She had laid out four settings of fruit and bread; the other two seats sat empty.

"Told you that girl was no good," she said.

"What are you talking about?" Johan asked.

"Still sleeping like that, in someone else's home and all. So rude. Other people just aren't made like you and me." She grabbed a loaf of bread and tore off a chunk without looking away from the door. "*I* wouldn't have been comfortable, that's for sure."

Johan tried not to look at his father's empty space. With the storm outside, he had no appetite. "What if she looked through his things?"

"She would have said something," his mother said. "We would have heard from her by now."

"But how can you know?"

"*Well go have a look yourself,*" she screamed as she slammed her hands down on the table.

Johan dropped the apple slice he'd been toying with and pushed his chair back. "Maybe I will," he said as he stepped away from the table.

"Go then," she said without as much as a glance.

Johan stared at her for a second before turning on his heel and heading for the stairs. He hit the top step and stopped. There was a noise coming from below that he didn't recognize. The only thing down there was storage; storage and Gwen.

Maybe she's up, he thought. *She can't have had a comfortable sleep.* He took the first step just as the front door blew in. The rain and wind nearly knocked him down the stairs as splinters of wood from the door frame flew through the hall. His mother screamed his name but Johan could barely hear her over the storm. He clung to the wall as bits of hail pelted his face and hands.

From the bottom of the stairs something growled. Johan tried to pull himself away but a chunk of ice the size of his fist slammed into his fingers. He lost his grip and the wind pushed him down to the basement. On the way down his legs flew above his head and he went head-first. He felt the crunch of bone as his shoulder slammed into the wooden step. He was airborne for just a moment before his face smashed into the concrete floor below.

Johan tried to pull himself upright but found nothing to grab hold of. One of his arms didn't work right; he used the other to wipe the flowing red veil from his eyes. Something was moving closer but no matter how much blood he wiped away he couldn't make his eyes focus.

"Johan," Gwen whispered.

"Gwen?" he shouted through the noise. "Help me Gwen, I can't see."

"You shouldn't have left me down here, Johan," she whispered. "You shouldn't have let me see. Now *you'll* see."

"Where are you?" he asked. "I can't see."

"Oh, you'll see," she said. "You'll *see.*" The storm had followed him to the basement; rain and hail beat down on him as it flooded the house. It washed the blood from his face but he wished it hadn't. Gwen stood before him, her long hair flying all around her. Her clothes were gone, but nothing feminine or human remained of her body.

Just below her breasts her skin had turned scaly. Dark tentacles grew where she once had arms. Her legs had merged into a slug-like strip of flesh that stretched back to the open storage room door. The skin of her face was gone, slick muscles flexing against white bone. Her hair hung limp around exposed jaws and cracked teeth. To Johan, she looked to be smiling.

He glanced past her and into the storage room. The crate had been pushed to the side, the forbidden hatch standing wide open. His father had gone down there once and never returned. His mother had covered it up and forbade entry ever since. Johan had never dared.

"Gwen," he said. "I'm sorry." As she stepped closer he squeezed his eyes closed. "I'm so, so sorry."

"Don't be," Gwen said. He heard a sucking sound as she moved closer. He turned his head to the side and waited for her to grab him, but as soon as one slimy tentacle touched his arm the screaming began.

Gwen let out an inhuman wail that shook the walls. He opened his eyes and saw what remained of his father standing between him and Gwen. His skin had been stripped away and his muscles looked like polished stone. He held one of his tools in his hand and screamed in a language Johan had never heard. His wild gray hair blew in the wind as he launched himself at Gwen.

"Johan," his mother screamed. She was at the top of the stairs calling to him. "Get out of there."

Johan leapt to his feet and fell on the stairs, his broken body unable to support his own weight. He screamed out in pain but it was drowned by the storm. As he clawed his way up, he snuck a glance down the hall.

His father had cut Gwen more times than Johan could count. Tentacles fell to the floor as her body separated into chunks of muscle and bone. She continued to scream up to the point where Johan's father separated her head from her torso. The basement turned shockingly quiet and the winds and rain died down to nothing. Puddles of blood and rainwater pooled at Johan's feet.

From behind, his mother grabbed him by the shoulders and tried to pull him up the stairs. They made it only a few feet up before his father turned and looked at them. He was without expression. His face lacked emotion. He stepped towards the stairs and looked at them.

Johan's mother passed out. She fell on top of Johan and they both tumbled to the bottom of the stairs.

***

Johan woke to pain. He stared at the darkness and tried to focus on one of the many shapes that moved around him. He couldn't move; everything hurt.

"You'll be fine in no time," his mother said. He tried to speak but his lips would not part. "I'll make you some soup. How'd that be?"

He could not respond, but his sight did start to return.

"No," she said. "Maybe not."

He could just make out his mother's face. Something moved all around her, almost like a dark aura. He lay in a bed, but it was not his own.

"You'll be just fine," she whispered. "Just fine." She reached up and gently pulled the bandages from his head. Little by little, the surrounding cavern became clear. Shapes moved in the distance, great beings that towered over everything else in sight. Surrounding the bed was a collection of tools that he couldn't hope to identify. His father was nearby, reading from his binder and chanting in a low voice.

His mother was smiling. Her skin had been removed and her hair whipped through the air like snakes. Her teeth had been ground down to sharp-looking nubs. "Your father's been here all along," she said. "He just needed his binder."

Johan reached up and felt his face. His hand came away sticky and red. He looked down and saw only tentacles where his arms and legs had been. He made them move. It felt nice. He glanced over at his father.

His mother ran a finger across his cheek and stood. "It looks like the family is back together again," she said. "And just in time for the holidays."

Johan smiled. *Family.*

"Things will be fine from now on," his mother said.

Of course they will, Johan thought. *They'll be fine from now on. Just fine.*

THE CURSED
Lawrence Salani

Lawrence lives on the coast near Sydney Australia. Writing horror stems from reading pulp writers of the past, main influences being H.P. Lovecraft, William Blake and Austin Spare. As well as writing he enjoys fine arts /painting and drawing. He finds that poetry assists with the creative process; however, his work seems to lean towards the darker tones. His published works include *A Fragment of Yesterday*, *Eclecticism E-Zine issue 5*, *Summer Heat*, *Night Terrors* anthology, Blood Bound Books, *The Angel of Death*, *Danse Macabre*, Edge publishing, *A Light in The Darkness*, *Darkness Ad Infinitum* and *Villipede*.

Insidious horror in the earth it doth lie,
Forever living, refusing to die.
A full moon caressed by rotting trees.
The scent of dead flesh floats on the breeze.

The soil is poison with eternal hate.
To walk on this ground a pernicious fate.
Evil crawls in the cold, black night;
Seeking flesh, but refusing the light.

Abhorrent horror with eyes that burn
In the dark night; a hunger doth yearn
To fulfill its sad destiny,
Between life and death for eternity.

Crouching in shadow, seeking its prey,
Released from its grave until the new day.
To run with horrors that cavort in the night;
Black daemons and ghouls, witches in flight.

The smell of warm flesh, alone in the dark;

An unearthly sound that freezes the heart.
The body grows limp with the tingle of fear,
The rustling of night owls as something grows near.

Frozen in wonder the sight to behold;
From shadows comes madness, its prey to enfold.
In the fetid darkness, lunatic screams go unheard.
Effulgent moon watches a scene so absurd.

Twisted trees glow in ethereal moonlight;
Hell's daemons look on with rapturous delight.
A myriad of stars shine in the sky;
Eternity beckons, time slowly drifts by.

Fear in your eyes, the first rays of the sun.
Crawl back to your grave when your work has been
        done.
Inside the foul earth your curse is to slumber,
Until darkness, again, doth summon your hunger.

GIFTS FROM A GRIM GODFATHER
Cathy Smith

Cathy Smith is a Mohawk of the Turtle Clan, and has lived all her life on a Status Indian Reservation on the Canadian Side of the border. She is proud of her people's culture and traditions, but is also interested in the cultures and traditions of other peoples, and she feels that speculative stories are myths of the modern age.

Joe Singer was becoming living proof that doctors made the worst patients. After a week of enforced bed rest he was feeling bored and restless. He had to concede that the diagnosis of over-exhaustion must've been correct because it was a full week before he noticed that his hospital bed wasn't comfortable. He'd been too tired to care, but now he was energetic enough to notice so he constantly shifted his weight and sat up in an effort to get comfortable.

There was nothing worth watching on T.V. so he looked over the get-well gifts he'd received. Most of them were cards, flowers and balloons from family, friends, colleagues and the occasional former patient. There was one that caught his eye. Everyone else had made the effort to make sure their gifts were cheery, and out in the open, but this one was in a plain white box. When he opened it he found a black hourglass with his name engraved in gold. His brow furrowed and he spent several moments looking for a card, anything that would tell him who gave him the hourglass.

When he found the card he sighed, "Grisham."

Of course, it's from him, that explains everything. Or, it explained the lack of decoration on the box but that didn't explain what it contained. "What was he thinking?" Grisham usually put some thought into his gifts, but that didn't always help the recipient guess what his intentions were. Grisham could be very generous, but sometimes he seemed almost unaware about what was socially appropriate. (Joe suspected that Grisham would be diagnosed with Asperger's in this modern day and age, but back in his time his odd behavior was accepted as him being Grisham.)

135

"Maybe old age is starting to make his brain foggy…" Grisham had been his grandfather's friend and it would only be natural that his faculties would start to slow down.

Joe could still remember the awkwardness as he looked down at the guitar in his hands. He wished he felt grateful, but knew this fine instrument would only go to waste. He must've looked at it too long because the old man asked, "Did I buy the right brand?" It was all Joe could do not to shudder when his eyes meant Grisham's. Grisham was so old it was scary. His face was so thin that the skull was readily apparent with eyes so black that in certain light the sockets looked empty. It didn't help that up to that point he'd only seen Grisham at the Singer family wakes and funerals, always looking dour and dressed in black, but this time was a festive occasion, his 12th birthday party.

It was all he could do not to squirm as those black eyes skewered him. An unfortunate side effect of their color was that it was hard to tell the iris from the pupil, and it had the effect of making whatever he gazed on the focus of over-intense interest.

Joe sought a polite lie and found it. "I was just thinking it'll be a while before I can start using it. I have to bring my math grades up—." Before he could stop himself he rambled on, "—especially if I want to be a doctor."

"So you're a Singer who wants to be a doctor?" Grisham asked. "It'll be a break from the family tradition." (Joe's family often said that Grisham was their "patron" and it wasn't much of an exaggeration.)

"I know my grandpa and father are musicians. Am I the only one Singer who's ever wanted something different?"

"The first Singer was a bard in the Old Country," Grisham said.

This was the first time Joe had heard about his family's history, but it wouldn't be the last, "You know a lot about my family, Grisham."

"More than any man living."

Joe gripped the guitar, and held it, "I'll make sure the guitar doesn't go to waste."

"If you haven't the desire to be a musician I won't force you to take lessons. A medical doctor is an honorable profession. I'll help you when the time comes," Grisham said.

Joe blinked. "Why would you do that?"

"I'm your godfather. It's my duty to help you prepare to earn a living with a trade."

Joe's brows drew together. This was the first time he heard that Grisham was his godfather, and what a godfather's duties were. "I didn't know being a godfather was like that."

"It's an old custom, and I'm old fashioned…"

Grisham played it safe with cards and money for birthday gifts from then on, but Joe was still shocked when he discovered just how generous his godfather could be.

The day of Joe's high school graduation should have been a joyous occasion, and had been until the letter arrived to turn it into the most depressing day of his life.

He'd gone off to the kitchen to be alone when Grisham intercepted him. "I thought graduations made people happy? You look like you're at a funeral—."

Joe couldn't trust himself to speak so he gave Grisham the letter. Grisham read the letter but merely shrugged and folded it up. "You didn't get a scholarship."

Joe would've exploded at the dismissive tone in Grisham's voice if the old man's next actions didn't shock him into silence. Grisham opened up his jacket, and took a cheque book out of his pocket. He proceeded to write in it. He ripped a cheque out from the book, and handed it to Joe. Joe gaped at the amount. He'd received cheques from Grisham before, but it'd only been pocket money on his birthday, nothing like this—.

"This should be sufficient for the first year's tuition and board."

"You're giving this to me?" Joe gasped.

"I told you I'd help you when the time came. The time is now. You'll get the next year's tuition cheque when I receive your grades," Grisham said.

"How can I thank you—."

The black eyes narrowed, "Get passing grades or I'll come to collect the money I gave you in full." Later on Joe convinced himself that Grisham was joking, but at that moment he couldn't help but shudder.

Every year he submitted a progress report to Grisham's lawyers. A cheque would be promptly sent out to cover the cost of next year's tuition and board. This was the process through pre-med and med school. He was the only one he knew who didn't graduate with school loan debt.

He didn't see Grisham again until his internship. He was simply too busy with his studies to attend many Singer family gatherings. He was making the rounds when he was startled by a dark figure in a hospital room. A shadow seemed to move by itself, but he calmed down when he realized it was a man in black at the foot of a bed. A moment later he realized the man was familiar to him, it was Grisham. "I'm sorry you startled me," he said because he'd let a cry out when he saw the shadow move.

"I was just visiting."

Joe checked the patient's chart. "You know Mr. Anderson?" He glanced at the comatose man hooked up to machines in the bed. "He's not in much of a position to appreciate your visit."

"I'm at an age where most of the people I know are dead or dying."

"Oh—."

"Since we're both here I might as well congratulate you. You're father told me you're planning on getting married in six months," Grisham said.

"I'll make sure you get an invite."

Grisham held up his hands, "Don't bother, Joseph. It's much too festive an occasion for me. I wouldn't know what to do with myself. But I still want to give you your wedding present."

This time Joe was the one who held up his hands, "No, you've already been too generous—."

"I like to see the Singer line continue. They're my favorite people in the world. I want to help you and your bride start out." He took an envelope out a pocket, and handed it to Joe. "Consider this a housewarming gift."

Joe's mouth fell open when he opened the envelope. The cheque was enough to cover the cost of a new home.

The only common thread Joe could see in his godfather's gifts was that he meant them to be useful. Joe glanced at the hourglass.

"What use could I possibly get from this hourglass or is he trying to lighten up, and give me a gag gift?"

Joe pondered the question for a while, but thanks to his fatigue his curiosity wasn't able to keep him up for long. His sleep was so deep and black that he lost all track of time, but when he woke up someone was looking down at him. He gasped. "Oh—it's you—Grisham."

Joe adjusted his bed so he could sit up and be more hospitable. "Thanks for your gift. It was—unique."

"It was meant to be symbolic."

"Symbolic?" Joe asked.

"Of my true gift to you, Joseph," Grisham said. He grabbed the hourglass and pressed it into Joe's hands. "Look at the hourglass."

Joe obeyed. For the first time he noticed that the sand was going very fast. "Is it a minute timer? It's big enough for me to expect it to go longer but it's going so fast."

"It's your life." Grisham said.

"My life?" Joe asked.

"This hourglass is a visible representation of your lifespan. It's meant to show you the effect your decisions have on your health," Grisham said.

"You're telling me I need to slow down?"

"I'll leave it for you to decide. It's not my job to tell people how to spend their lives, but since you're a Singer I'm giving you this warning," Grisham sighed.

"Job?"

"I am Death, Joseph."

"Death?" Joe's brows came together. "You're Death?"

Grisham closed his eyes, "Yes."

Grisham wasn't completely humorless but his humor was extremely dry almost to the point of blackness.

"Why would Death agree to be anyone's godfather?" Joe asked.

"I already told you—the Singers are my favorite people in the world."

"What makes Singers so special to you? Are we your pets?"

"A bard had the audacity to serenade me during the time of the Black Death. I became curious and got attached to him, and his descendants since then."

"You're serious about this? You knew the first Singer?" Joe asked, shaking his head.

"I've been the Singers' family friend for generations," Grisham said.

For one terrifying instant Joe looked at those perennially sharp black eyes, and believed him, but then he started to laugh, "Death has enough money to pay to send his godson to med school?"

"I've had ages to build my resources, Joseph."

"You paid for me to become a doctor, and save lives. Doesn't that go against everything you stand for?"

Grisham shrugged. "Lives don't stay saved, Joseph. It matters little to me whether I get to collect a soul sooner or later, but I'd rather collect a Singer later."

"Because we're your favorite people in the world?"

"I could've taken you when you collapsed. I would've if you were anyone but a Singer, but I'm letting you off with a warning—."

Joe wasn't even paying attention to Grisham anymore. He kept muttering to himself, "The doctors are right...I've been working too hard...I must be hallucinating...I need to rest..."

Seeing that he wasn't going to convince Joe otherwise Grisham sighed.

"I'll let you believe what you want to believe, Joseph, but I'm leaving you that hourglass. We'll see each other again when the sand runs out."

Joe woke up by himself, but the hourglass was running beside his bed, and as long as he was able to look at it, it kept on running.

ABOUT

Founded in 2010, Burial Day Books is a boutique publisher of supernatural horror. Burial Day Books publishes works by emerging and established horror authors monthly, as well as publishes a yearly anthology, the *Gothic Blue Book*.

Cynthia (cina) Pelayo is the owner of Burial Day Books. Her works include the short story collection, *Loteria*, and her novel, *Santa Muerte* which was nominated for an International Latino Book Award. Pelayo's short stories have appeared in The Horror Zine, Danse Macabre, MicroHorror, Seedpod Publishing, Static Movement, Flashes in the Dark, among other publications. Her nonfiction work has appeared in Gozamos, Time Out, Extra Bilingual News, Venus Zine, FNews and Atlas Obscura. She currently lives in Chicago with her husband and her son. For more about her, visit cinapelayo.com or follow her on Twitter @cinapelayo.

Gerardo Pelayo is a photographer, a programmer, a baseball enthusiast, a lover of good barbecue and the manager of all things technical at Burial Day Books. Follow Gerardo on Twitter at @Thee_Undertaker.